Winter's
End

Winter's End

by Catherine Storr

Harper & Row, Publishers
New York, Hagerstown, San Francisco, London

FIRST AMERICAN EDITION

Library of Congress Cataloging in Publication Data
Storr, Catherine.
  Winter's end.

  SUMMARY: An old family house has a mysterious effect
on a group of teenagers staying there.
  [1. England—Fiction] I. Title.
PZ7.S8857Wi   [Fic]   78-19488
ISBN 0-06-026069-6
ISBN 0-06-026072-6 lib. bdg.

1

You had to drive for miles along twisting, narrow roads bordered by high hedges screening the country-side. You went through little villages, no more than a handful of houses and a bus stop. You went past scrub woods, around hairpin corners, then for three miles along a dead-straight road that the Romans might have built. Suddenly you'd have a view of fields on one side, where the hedge had been cut down to nothing. A whole flat earth, it seemed, of plowed bare fields, sodden, with rain in the furrows and no sign of life. Only the great arc of the sky, full of pale gray cumulus clouds, waiting to rain down and fill the ditches and trenches with more water. Then the hedge sprang up again and you were back with nothing but the road in front to look at.

Straight, bend, straight, curve, miniature crossroads, straight, bend. Like a dance. But boring with it.

"How much farther?" Cary asked.

"Not much. It's difficult to see. The map . . ."

"But you've been here before? I thought . . ."

Philip said, "Ages ago. I was six."

"Didn't it belong to your aunt? Or something?"

"Uncle."

"Why'd he leave it to you?"

"He didn't have any kids of his own. I only saw him that once. I don't know why he picked me," Philip said.

"You were a little golden-haired toddler and you did a Fauntleroy on him," Bran suggested.

"What's a Fauntleroy?" Cary asked.

"Little Lord. You must have heard of him. He sucked up to his hoary old grandfather and got to be heir to a great big estate. We had it read aloud to us in school," Bran said.

"No he didn't. He was the heir anyway, because of his father being the earl's son." Rosemary, as usual reliably factual.

"I didn't, anyway. I didn't ever see my uncle again. I told you." That was Philip.

"To hell with all this long-lost-heir stuff. Do I turn left or right?" Bran asked. They'd come to a crossroads and only two of the possible four ways were marked. One arm of the signpost pointed to Fetters, another to Winter Lacey. The other two roads were unposted.

"Straight on. I think."

Bran drove straight on. The road, narrower still,

began to run between hills, low at first, then higher. The short day's light was already half gone. Rosemary, looking out into the dusk, felt enclosed, shut in.

Philip said suddenly, "Here!" The car drew up before a gateway. Tall brick posts, each surmounted by a stone globe. Evergreens lined the narrow way beyond. There were no gates.

"I remember this. It's all right," Philip said.

Bran drove his ancient mini up the drive. The humped ground between the ruts was grassed over. Not many cars had come this way lately. The two girls in the back looked out at the dark, glossy leaves of rhododendrons flanking the roadway. At the pale stems of birches and the black pine needles beyond. Cary took out a pocket mirror and tidied her smooth hair. Rosemary looked at the back of Bran's head and wished she could see inside it and find out what he was thinking. She thought she knew, and she wasn't sure that she liked it.

"This it?" Bran asked, bringing the mini to a halt where the drive came out of the overgrowth of shrubs into the open. Rosemary could see white stone steps, the bottom of a wall.

Philip said, "Yes. This is it."

He sounded embarrassed. Rosemary understood that and was sorry for him. She'd known, when they'd discussed going away as a group for a sort of working holiday this spring, that he'd found it difficult to let on that he owned a house in the country. Actually owned it. He was afraid that it would make him too much different from the other undergraduates. He'd appear a capitalist, a property owner. One of them out there, the oppressors, on the other side. Poor old Philip. Anything less like an oppressive type Rosemary couldn't imagine. She felt kind towards him. He couldn't help it if his uncle had left him a house. And he was doing his best, sharing with his friends.

She followed Cary out of the car and, looking up, was astonished. She didn't know exactly what she'd expected. A cottage, perhaps, with half-timbers and a thatched roof. Possibly a run-down Victorian vicarage, like the one near Winchester where her aunt had a flat. Whatever she could have imagined, it wouldn't have been like this . . . this graceful, composed pale palace in miniature, gleaming white in the growing dusk like a shell against dark water. Wide steps led up to a front door under a little portico, supported on slender white pillars. On each side of the portico were long windows, narrow oblongs of blank panes breaking, in perfect symmetry, the expanse of the white facade. The larger window over the portico was gently rounded above, in contrast to the elegant little straight balustrade which bordered the roof.

Rosemary felt for Philip more than ever. She saw Bran, straightening up from lifting grips out of the car boot, take his first real look at the house. She heard his "Phew!" on a long, indrawn breath. She heard Cary say, in her soft sweet voice, "Phil, it's beautiful! You didn't say how fantastically beautiful it was." Philip didn't answer this directly. He said, almost as if he were apologizing, "I've got the keys somewhere." He found them, mounted the steps, and tried the door. It opened inwards, and he held it open for Cary to enter first. He said, "I just hope it's all right."

All right wasn't the expression for it. Rosemary had never seen another house like it in real life, only on the screen.

The front door opened directly into the square hall, lit by a glass dome overhead; a wide, curving staircase led up to the balconied corridor running around three sides of the square on the upper floor. The walls were paneled in a pale gray-painted wood. The floors were slippery pale boards on which lay, at spaced intervals, pale, washed Oriental carpets. Pale engravings in slim ebony frames hung on the walls above the stairs.

Doors, also gray, led off in different directions. Philip opened one to the left of the front door, and they looked in at a long drawing room, the sofas and chairs shrouded in dust sheets. There were windows in all three outer walls; those at the farther end were French windows opening into a conservatory, its large ornamental pots standing empty under the staring glass roof. Bran pressed the light switches by the door, and the room sprang into brilliant illumination. Two crystal chandeliers hanging from the high ceiling dazzled their eyes, accustomed to the muted daylight; a wall cupboard, lit by internal strip lighting, showed china, white and gold, the plates standing up, the cups tilted on their saucers, for display, not for use. In the marble fireplace, the polished knobs of the fire irons reflected back the glittering diamond drops of the chandeliers. On little tables scattered along the room were small, precious objects: alabaster boxes, china bowls waiting for potpourri, enameled ashtrays, a plate of smooth eggs of semiprecious stones. On a half-circle side table was a collection of Victorian glass paperweights, each transparent dome imprisoning a cluster of bright patterned colors. The impression was of the Sleeping Beauty's palace. Treasures everywhere, perfect order, no dust, no dirt. Everything waiting for life to be breathed into it.

"Christ! When did . . . ? How long has the place been empty?" Bran asked. He clicked off the switches as they left the drawing room. Philip led the way across the hall and opened the opposite door. He said, "It's been empty since December. Three months. But there's a caretaker."

"Living here, d'you mean?" Rosemary could understand Bran's astonishment. It didn't feel like a lived-in house. More like a well-kept museum.

"I don't think so. I think she comes in from the village."

"Old family retainer?" Bran asked, and then thought, too late, that this might have sounded like a sneer. To hell with the class system, he thought; why couldn't he forget that Philip came from what he supposed his grandmother would have called the gentry? Why couldn't he just accept Philip as a nice guy—which he was—to whom education in a sort of private school, professional parents, and the ownership of this extraordinary house were as much accidents as winning the pools or becoming an international football star? To correct what might

6

have seemed like sniping, he said, "Is it like you remembered?"

Philip looked around the room they were standing in. It was a dining room, half the size of the long room they'd just left, but equally grand, with heavy green curtains drawn back from the long windows, a huge mahogany table and chairs, and a sideboard loaded with cut glass. He said, "I'm not sure. It seemed enormous. But I was smaller, so I suppose it all looked bigger then."

"Looks big enough to me now," Bran said.

"What happens at the back? D'you know?" Cary asked.

They walked around the curved staircase, over the pale carpets, to another door at the back of the house. It opened on a long slim room, running across the width of the building. Shaded lights, hanging low over great stuffed leather chairs, showed walls solid with shelves, each one stacked full of cloth- and leather-backed books, with not a space to be seen. There were tables topped by tooled leather, brass ashtrays, and a pair of library steps of light oak. You could reach to the topmost shelf of the tall room if you stood on the top step. But none of the books looked as if they had been disturbed for a hundred years. Or as if they wanted to be read. Like the china in the drawing room, they were there for show.

Bran sniffed.

"Damp."

"Is that what it is?" Philip asked.

"I rather like it. Smells like my gran's Sunday-school

prizes always did. Old. She'd not read them in fifty years." He vividly remembered putting his small nose into the opened pages of an old-fashioned book with small print in double columns, and at the same time he could almost feel the texture of the bunched woolen skirt his gran always wore, and he heard her voice saying, "Never had time to read them though."

He came back to the present with a start. They were back in the hall and Cary was speaking. "I think it's all lovely! Lucky you!" she was saying, her eyes making up to Philip, admiring him for the beauty of his possessions. She said, "Let's look upstairs, shall we? We'll have to decide who's going to sleep where."

They went up the shallow steps of the curved staircase and saw an array of pale doors opening off the balcony. The first that Cary opened, at the head of the stairs, showed a typical Victorian bedroom: The chintz of the bedspread and upholstery matched the blues and grays of the flowered wallpaper, the fitted carpet, and the long curtains. The head and foot of the single bed were of solid, dark mahogany. There were blue vases on the white mantelpiece, and between them a gray clock with its hands neatly set at twelve o'clock. Everything was exquisitely clean and tidy. The room felt as if it had been empty for a long time.

The next door led into what had obviously once been a dressing room. A huge Victorian tub stood out from one wall on lion's legs, looking strangely naked and lost, and the lavatory, at a considerable distance, with a polished wooden seat and overhanging cistern, seemed equally ill at ease. Both looked wrong to people used to seeing their modern counterparts squeezed into the smallest possible space. Could you ever use either of them and feel quite safe? Rosemary wondered. It would be like sleeping in a bunk bed alone in the middle of a desert. You'd never be able to fall asleep with so much emptiness all around you.

Behind the next door was a broom cupboard big enough, Bran said, to house his mini. They moved on to the cross corridor, running the width of the house. The first door opened into another bedroom, a larger replica of the other, except that here the chintz was purplish rather than blue, and there were two wide bedsteads with brass heads and feet, side by side. Again the absolute order. Again the emptiness.

It was the next room which was different. It was even bigger, twice the size of its neighbor. Even so it was dominated by the immense four-poster bed which stood against the middle of one wall. It had twisted pillars of black oak and it was draped with crimson. A crimson rug lay on the white carpeted floor in front of the empty grate, and two more ran by the sides of the bed. The effect should have been warm, but instead it was forbidding. The two windows, curtained with the same crimson, must look towards the hills behind the house, but at this moment their black panes only reflected back the interior of the room, making it seem even larger. Rosemary took an instant dislike to it. The grandeur and stateliness downstairs hadn't seemed wrong, if a little overwhelming, but the formality of this bedroom was against comfort.

"Fantastic!" Cary said.

Rosemary shivered.

"You cold?" Bran asked.

"Not really. I don't think. Yes. Perhaps I am."

"Let's just see where everything is," Cary said. She opened the third door and they saw a bare, uncarpeted passage leading off from the back of the house. "Servants' wing," Cary said complacently, and Bran, noticing Philip's look of discomfort, pitied him for Cary's insensitive snobbery. He could imagine that Cary would enjoy having servants to order about, to needle with heavy-handed patronage. But no one had occupied these rooms for decades, that was clear. There were dust sheets over empty beds, and the windows were curtainless. Deal stairs with no carpet, at the end of the wing, led back to the ground floor.

They returned to the main part of the house and examined the remaining rooms. Two more bathrooms, one fairly modern, two more chintzy bedrooms, led off the third side of the balcony. Philip said, as if he were grateful they'd come to the end, "That's all."

"It's great! It's really great! It's like a palace," Cary said.

"Plenty of room," Bran said.

"It's funny, though . . ." Rosemary began.

"What's funny?" Cary was sharp.

"There doesn't seem to be a nursery. You'd think . . ."

"It was probably in the wing at the back," Cary said impatiently.

"But there weren't . . ." Rosemary tried to remember

what it was that hadn't been there. How could you notice something that was missing? She felt the familiar discomfort of searching for a tiny memory that constantly slipped away just out of reach. Cary had said, "Well, anyway . . ." when she caught up with it. "There aren't any bars!"

"*Bars*?"

"Window bars. So that babies can't fall out."

Philip looked at her, frowning, as if he were puzzled. Bran smiled. Cary said, "You couldn't have window bars in a house like this! They'd completely spoil it. Unless it was right at the back. Anyway, I think it's perfect," Cary said.

"Not so bad," Bran said.

"What about the rooms? Who wants to be where?" Philip asked, as if, Bran thought, to show he wasn't going to play the proprietor, he wanted them all to share.

"I'd love for us to have the room with the four-poster. I've always wanted to sleep in one. If . . ." Cary said. Rosemary noticed her use of the word "us." Cary was taking it for granted, then, that she and Philip would be sharing a room. Which meant that there'd be the more pressure put on her to share with Bran. And she didn't know whether that was what she wanted. She certainly didn't want to be rushed. She needed time to consider. She hadn't made up her mind yet whether she would or she wouldn't sleep with him.

"If what?" Philip asked.

"It's only . . . Do you remember which was your uncle's room?" Cary said.

11

"Not really. It's such ages. Anyway, what's that got to do with the four-poster room?"

Cary said, "I just wondered. I mean, I wouldn't want to sleep in the bed he'd . . . You know. The one he'd died in."

Philip began, "I . . ." at the same moment as Bran said, "If you can't sleep in a bed someone's died in, you'd better take a sleeping bag around with you. Someone'll have died in every bed in a house this old."

"No, but . . . Phil's uncle's only just died. . . ."

"You mean you don't mind if someone died in the bed twenty years ago, but if it's only last year you do?" Bran said, thinking of his gran, whom he'd seen as a child dying by stages and hating it, yet never losing her dignity. And the day after the funeral he and his brother had moved into the room she'd always had. He remembered saying to his dad, scared, and yet more scared of being laughed at as a ninny, "Gran can't come back?" His dad hadn't laughed. He'd said, "She won't. What she needs now's a long rest." He'd been reassured, after the first night hadn't thought about how Gran had died in the bed he was sharing with Johnny. In no time at all it had become the place where he and Johnny fought for their fair half share, where they bickered, where they dreamed, where at various moments in the long process of growing up there seemed always to be one person too many for one or the other of them. Where they'd also exchanged secret, shameful information they'd discovered from their own experiences or those of other boys and later, of course, of girls. Very soon, if he thought about his gran at all, it was with a sort of loving guilt that he didn't think about her more. He said, roughly, "I suppose you think death is catching?" and saw Cary's eyes turn to him, uncomprehending and half angry, half frightened. But Rosemary, standing behind her, knew what he meant. "Yes," she thought, "it is like that. We don't like talking about dying, we pretend it doesn't happen. Just as if it were infectious, and if we get close to it we might find it was happening to us."

She heard Philip say, "Anyway, this was the spare room," and saw Cary's pretty smile as she said, "That's all right, then. Let's have it, shall we?" She put a hand on Philip's arm and looked at him in the way Rosemary disliked so much. "Cary's appealing look" was how she thought of it. Cary used it on anyone when she wanted something. She'd have used it on Rosemary if she'd thought it would work.

Philip hesitated. He said, "What about the others? Anyone else putting in for the four-poster?"

Rosemary's "No!" came out more explosively than she'd meant it to. Cary stared at her.

Bran said, "I don't want a four-poster," and Philip said to Cary, "All right. You have it, then." Making it over to her. He said to Rosemary, "Which room would you like?"

"The little one at the far end." It was the farthest she could get from Cary, and she'd seen that it contained only one, single bed.

"Bran? What about the room the other side of the

bathroom next to Rosemary?" Philip didn't say where he himself meant to sleep. He said, "When the others come we may have to reshuffle. There'll be six of us and there are only five bedrooms. Some of us'll have to double up."

"Might be a good idea," Bran said. The room he'd been allotted had two beds. Rosemary knew that he wasn't looking at her on purpose and felt that she flushed, then was furious herself for being so conscious.

"Why six? Is your Jamie bringing someone else with him?" Cary asked.

"He's bringing his sister."

"His *sister*? What on earth does he want to bring a sister for?"

"I didn't understand properly. Something about their parents being away from home and he couldn't leave her on her own."

"How old is she?" Cary asked sharply.

"Quite a bit younger than he is. I've met her at their house. She must be thirteen. Fourteen. Something like that."

"Christ! A kid! What made you agree, Phil? She'll be a hellish nuisance. We are supposed to be working, aren't we? Not looking after a ruddy kid."

"I couldn't very well say she couldn't come. After all, there's plenty of room here. And Jamie seemed to think she could amuse herself all right when we're working."

"Kids that age never stop talking," Cary said.

"She doesn't talk. I've hardly ever heard her say a word."

14

"I just hope she keeps quiet here," Cary said. Rosemary thought enviously, "God, she's beautiful even when she's bad tempered," and felt how unfair it was that Cary had everything. Long hair the color of a burnished chestnut skin new out of its prickly husk; gray eyes with long dark lashes, beautifully shaped dark eyebrows, and a fantastic figure. She was like one of those heroines you read about in women's magazines, sometimes fictional, sometimes real-life heroines, who look right in whatever clothes they happen to wear. Beside her, Rosemary felt too short, too well covered, uncoordinated, plain. She supposed that she ought to be grateful that Bran preferred her to Cary, and she was, in a way. But that didn't make him inevitably the right person for her. It only complicated her feelings about him. She sighed. Life was complicated. Sometimes she wondered how she would ever get through another fifty years of it without making the most horrible mistakes. Look at this working holiday, for instance! She was worried enough about next term's exams; then on top of that she would have, sooner or later, to make up her mind what she felt about Bran. And now there was going to be an unknown teenage girl with whom she, Rosemary, would undoubtedly be burdened. "I'm sure to get landed with her. It's what always happens to my sort of person," she thought.

They went back down the curling staircase again to fetch their various pieces of luggage. Cary's of course was elegant and new looking, and Philip carried it up for her when she put on her fragile air of finding it too heavy even to lift, let alone get up a flight of stairs. As

15

Rosemary took her own shabby, elderly suitcase into the small room she'd chosen, she heard Cary's voice. "You'll bring your case in here, won't you, Phil?" Making sure he didn't escape. There were still two more rooms, unoccupied until the day after tomorrow. He could firmly take one of those. Rosemary heard a door shut, but didn't know whose, or whether Philip was alone behind it.

She wondered what it was going to be like here with these people whom she'd met for the first time only six months ago, at the beginning of the college year in October. Philip? She'd liked him at once. She'd found his friendly shyness attractive. It had reassured her that she wasn't the only first-year student to feel strange and a little frightened at finding herself living away from home for the first time, and unsure of how far she'd be able to cope with the academic standards. Cary she'd recognized on sight as likely to be the pinup girl of the year. She'd been proved right there. Apart from the sort of social encounters arising from their use of the communal baths and kitchen, she hardly knew her. She had, however, in spite of not wanting Philip as a boyfriend herself, felt a trace of disappointment when she'd seen him, in this last term, gradually succumb to Cary's insistent pursuit. And Bran? Bran she'd also only really got to know this last term. She didn't want to examine yet what she felt about Bran. He was different from anyone else she knew. That was as far as she'd go for the moment.

She unpacked quickly. The room was very cold, and though there was a small electric fire she didn't like to turn it on for the short time she'd be there. She hoped there'd be somewhere warmer downstairs, and as soon as she could she went down to prospect. Sounds from behind a door to the left of the bottom of the stairs led her to investigate. She found herself in a large, surprisingly modern-looking kitchen, with a big, scrubbed wooden table, shelves full of pots and pans, and what she gratefully thought of as ordinary plates and cups and saucers. Dishes meant to be used, not just looked at. There was a cream-colored stove, a kind she didn't recognize, a wicker chair with a red cushion, a tiled floor, and a double sink. She exclaimed. Bran, who was kneeling on the floor in front of the stove, and Philip, who was standing at the table looking into a large cardboard carton, looked at her. Bran said, "What's up?"

"Nothing. It's just that this room's different from the rest of the house."

"It's just as cold. I'm sorry," Philip said.

"Stop apologizing. It isn't your fault. Anyway, once I've got this thing going, it won't be cold in here. Heats the water, too," Bran said.

"What is it?" Rosemary asked. She looked over Bran's shoulder at an array of taps and clockfaces. "How do you know what to do?"

"My mum's got one the same kind. Rayburn. Smashing. This is another model, but I should be able to work out how it goes. In a minute or two."

"Can you cook on it?" Rosemary asked.

"Course you can. Only not when it's only just been lighted. Tomorrow."

"Then what about supper tonight?"

"There's a little electric thing. A hot plate and an oven. Only it's tiny," Philip said.

"Can you cook?" Bran asked Rosemary.

"I can . . ."

"You don't sound very sure."

"I can do ordinary things. I'm not very good."

There was a satisfying crackle going on inside the Rayburn. Bran said, "That's it! Now we'll be all right. Or we will tomorrow. You'll see."

He got up from his knees and went over to the carton on the table.

"I'll cook tonight, if you like. What've we got?"

"Who sent it?" Rosemary asked.

"There's a note on top. Just says, 'Groceries to be going on with. Hope you're comfortable,' " Philip said.

"Your caretaker?" Bran asked.

"It's signed N. Rammage. I thought the caretaker was called something different."

"Never mind who it was. Tell me what we've got," Bran said, washing his hands at the sink.

Whoever N. Rammage was, he or she had thought of almost everything they might need for a first, picnic meal. Bread, butter, cheese, milk; a tin of tuna fish, another of minced beef. Tea, instant coffee. Digestive biscuits, a packet of spaghetti, a tube of tomato puree. Apples, oranges, onions. Bran was frying some of the onions on top of the electric plate, while Rosemary grated cheese and Philip discovered plates, knives and forks, a salt cellar, and a peppermill, when the kitchen door opened and Cary came in. She began, "Phil . . ." but broke off to say , "Onions! Fantastic! I'm ravenous. What're you making?" to Bran.

"Spaghetti Napolitana. Or is it Bolognese? I can never remember which is which."

"Aren't you clever? I didn't know you were a cook."

"I'm not 'a cook.' I just cook when I need to, that's all." Bran's voice said that he didn't care for Cary's flattery. She turned back to Philip.

"You haven't unpacked yet. Shall I do it for you?"

"It's all right, thanks. I'll do it later," Philip said.

"Go on," Bran urged him in his mind. "Stand up to her, tell her you're a big boy now, you can unpack for yourself." But his thoughts had no more effect than such thoughts usually do. Philip said nothing more, and Cary said, "No, I'll do it. Won't take me a minute." She was off. They heard her footsteps running up the stairs. If Rosemary hadn't been there, carefully not looking at anyone, Bran would have said right out, "Why don't you tell her to mind her own business?" But he couldn't betray masculine solidarity. So instead he said, "Supper'll be ready in another twenty minutes. With luck." This had the effect he'd meant. Philip said unhappily, "I'd better just go and see what's happening," and left.

"Is that enough cheese?" Rosemary asked.

"My god! You didn't grate the lot?" Bran said, looking at the soup bowl piled high.

"You didn't say how much. I thought you wanted all of it grated."

"Must have been about a pound. It's only for the

topping. What on earth made you go on like that?"

"I didn't know it was only for the top. You might have been going to cook some too."

"Doesn't matter. It'll taste just the same grated as whole. Now. Where's the tin of mince?"

The tin was an awkward shape and the tin opener which they found in the kitchen drawer was of a variety unknown to either of them. "Like an intelligence test," Bran grumbled, turning it this way and that trying to make out how it worked.

"If that's an intelligence test, I must be an idiot. I can't see it at all," Rosemary said.

"That's silly. You're not trying."

"But even if I tried I wouldn't be able to make it work."

Bran exploded. "Don't be so feeble! Why the hell do you take it for granted that you couldn't do it as well as anyone else? Of course you could if you made up your mind to it. You're so bloody afraid of making an ass of yourself. . . . Damn!" The tin opener had suddenly worked and too well. It had taken a small and bloody chunk out of his thumb. He sucked it.

"Hold it under the cold tap," Rosemary said.

The thumb flowed bloody water.

"Thumbs have a good blood supply. Did you know?" Bran asked.

"Now I do." Rosemary was grateful to the thumb for diverting Bran's attention from her failings. He was probably right. She was frightened of failure, wanted to do things successfully or not at all. But she didn't like to be scolded. She asked, "How is it?"

"Bloody," Bran said, and laughed. "Got a bit of cotton wool?"

"Upstairs I have. I'll get it."

When she came down again, Bran was holding his left hand up in the air, gripping the base of the thumb with the fingers of his right hand.

"It's easing off. Got the cotton? Give me just a wee scrap, will you? Not as big as that, stupid. Really small. A whisk you can see through. That's better." He applied the whisk to the wound and Rosemary saw it turn pink, then red. Drops of blood oozed through.

"Another like that."

The second whisk did the trick. The thumb still looked bloody, but there were no more drops.

"Onions are burning," Rosemary said. She stirred the pan vigorously. "Tell me what to do next."

Bran wrapped his thumb in a piece of kitchen paper and bound it with an elastic band which had held a piece of paper around the onions. "Fill that big pan with water. Now stick it on the electric plate. The onions can wait for a bit. Must get the spaghetti cooked and drained."

Rosemary did what she was told. She felt comfortable with Bran like this, working together on a job, exchanging opinions on the taste of the sauce once Bran had got the mince, the tomato puree, and the onions all cooking together with the spaghetti gently drying off in the tiny oven. No emotional overtones. Or undertones.

She was thinking this, going to and fro between the

dresser and the table in the process of laying plates and cutlery, when Bran caught her arm as she passed him.

"Rosey?"

"What?"

"Like me?"

No difficulty in answering this. "Course I do."

"How much?"

This was more difficult. "I do like you, Bran."

"Fancy me?"

There was a distant thump overhead. Bran laughed. "D'you think that's Cary falling over with Philip on top of her? Venus and Adonis?"

"What's Venus and Ado . . . ?"

"She was keener than he was. Couldn't get him to the point, so she made a thing of falling over backwards and taking him with her. Shakespeare."

"You mean they . . . did it on the stage?" Rosemary asked.

"Christ! Didn't you know he wrote poems too?"

"I know about the sonnets. But I've only read some of them."

"*Venus and Adonis*. Sort of epic poem, I suppose. And that's education! Is that the salt? Give it to me, will you?" Bran said.

"Do you really think Cary would . . . ?"

"I don't know if she's really randy or just predatory. Poor old Philip."

"Why poor? Cary's terribly attractive. She's had lots of men after her. And he needn't have asked her to come here if he didn't like her. I mean, it isn't as if she was either of us's friend."

"Obvious she's not yours," Bran said and laughed.

"Do you like her?"

"Like? I don't think Cary's the sort of person you like. She's . . ." He stopped as the door opened and Cary came in, followed by Philip. Rosemary saw, resentfully, that Cary had changed into a long skirt. She was flushed and prettier than ever.

"It's freezing upstairs," she said.

"You look warm enough," Bran said.

"We put on the electric fire. But it is freezing all the same. It's cold down here, too."

"It'll be all right tomorrow when the stove's got going properly."

"Why didn't your caretaker light it for you? She knew when we were coming," Cary said to Philip.

Bran, carrying the saucepan full of spaghetti, shining with butter, over to the table where the others were sitting, said, "Funny of her to lay in food and not to light the Rayburn. Or didn't you ask her to?" He put generous helpings on each plate and turned back for the sauce.

"I didn't ask her to bring food, either. Never thought about it," Philip said.

"Of course not! Housekeeping isn't a man's business," Cary said at once.

Bran opened his mouth to ask why not, then decided that statements like that weren't worth taking seriously, and he put a forkful of his own cooking into his mouth instead. He was half amused, half annoyed to find that Cary was bent on exercising her charm on him that evening; probably an attempt to make Philip jealous. But he wouldn't play up to her, and after a time she gave up. They finished the meal with oranges and coffee in near-total silence. They were all tired and the kitchen was still not warm. Rosemary fetched yet another sweater and washed up. Cary stood by the draining board drying the dishes as they came out of the soapy water, yawning prodigiously. She and Rosemary didn't exchange a word.

"Any hot-water bottles?" Bran asked Philip.

"I brought my own. I'll fetch it," Cary said.

A brief search revealed several old-fashioned stone bottles. Rosemary filled them in turns from the electric kettle. When she'd done the last, she announced that she was going to bed. She was tired of Cary's ploys and didn't want, tonight, to find herself left alone downstairs with Bran. It didn't improve her feeling of strangeness to find that the sheets were lying in a neat laundered pile on the mattress. She made the bed crossly, wrapped the stone bottle in a cardigan, and got into bed hugging it. She felt chilled. Wasn't sure she didn't wish she'd never come. She heard footsteps in the passage outside and the sound of the plug in the bathroom next door. Eventually she had warmed up enough to sleep.

No one knocked on her door that night.

2

The next morning the kitchen was an oasis of warmth in the chilly desert of the rest of the house. They tried to work there, but it wasn't easy. Three of them needed room in order to spread textbooks and notes, and though the kitchen table was large, there wasn't as much space as they needed. Rosemary kept looking up from Johnson's *Lives of the Poets*, one of her set books and one she found boring, and looking out the window. Not because there was anything interesting to be seen outside. Nothing but the yard, and beyond the old stable block the tops of trees, bare and ghostly in the thin misty rain. Bran read, made notes, stretched, yawned, drew a diagram in his notebook and then crossed it out fiercely, read again. Philip's left hand fidgeted with the lock of

25

hair that fell over his forehead. He wasn't reading steadily either. Often when Rosemary looked up she saw his eyes fixed on Bran, on her, or, more often, on Cary. Cary, sitting in the wicker chair, was the only one of them who seemed able to concentrate without difficulty. This was annoying, too. Rosemary wanted some reasonable excuse for disliking her. If Cary had disturbed the others by talking or restlessness, there'd have been less shame in disliking her. "I'm envious," Rosemary thought. She'd envied Cary's looks often before; now she had to envy her powers of concentration too.

At midday, Bran pushed his books away from him.

"I can't do any more this morning. I'll go down to the village. Anyone want to come too?"

It was a relief not to have to pretend any longer to be working. Bran drove along the overgrown drive, back along the lane to the crossroads, and then turned right to Winter Lacey. The village lay at the bottom of the valley and it was small. There were two streets of cottages built of gray stone, three or four shops, and a bus shelter. That was about all. In the post office, which also sold knitting needles and wool, stationery, tobacco, and sweets, they bought postcards and stamps and asked how to order in milk, where to find sausages, fruit, more cheese, and eggs. They were directed to the greengrocers' on the opposite side of the street, and there, in front of shelves which seemed to hold an assortment of everything from washing powder to bananas and tinned salmon, was a rounded middle-aged woman, with bright blue eyes and very pink cheeks like pincushions each side of a stubby, humorous nose. The blue eyes ran over them with friendly curiosity as they came in. When she'd finished serving the only other customer in the shop, she asked, "You from Winter's End?"

It was Cary who said, "That's right."

"One of you two young men must be Mr. Edmund's nephew, then?"

"He is," Bran said, indicating Philip, who hadn't seemed ready to answer.

"I ought to've known. He's got the Edmund face. And the hair, too."

"Did you know the family?" Cary asked.

"I knew the last two Mr. Edmunds. Mr. Peter and Mr. Edward. I can't hardly remember Mr. Nicholas. He was before my day. I was only a child when he died. In nineteen twenty-five. My mother worked for him for a time before she married. And she used to go up sometimes to help in the house for Mr. Peter when he had guests. That'd have been before Mrs. Edmund died. His wife. After she went, he didn't entertain." The woman fixed her eyes on Cary's pretty, eager face. "You're not an Edmund?"

"No, I'm not." Cary made it sound as if she'd have liked nothing better than to be able to claim relationship. The woman looked at her again, then glanced at Rosemary and Bran. "I'd say none of you were family except him." She nodded towards Philip.

"That's right. We're just friends."

"All at college together?"

"Us four are. There's another coming tomorrow who's at Oxbridge."

"On holiday now, are you?"

"Sort of. We've come here on a reading party. Work."

"Working hard?" the woman asked, her bright eyes twinkling.

"Very hard," Bran said, laughing back.

"Well now! What can I get you? Do you want the things sent or will you be taking them?"

They'd made out a sort of list on their way down in the car. The woman suggested additions, and by the time they'd finished, there were two full cardboard boxes standing on the counter, and they'd spent nearly five pounds. As Bran heaved one up, the woman said, "You've got a car? I could send them up tonight after the shop's closed."

"It's all right. Car's outside," Bran called back over his shoulder.

Philip, in the act of lifting the second, was reminded of something. "Someone left a lot of stuff for us last night. Was it . . . ?"

"I thought you might not've remembered to bring much with you," the woman said.

"We hadn't brought hardly anything. It was great. But . . . I'm sorry, I don't know who you are. . . ."

"No reason why you should. You were only small when Mr. Peter brought you in here to see me. Nancy. Nancy Rammage. You won't remember . . ."

Philip said slowly, "You had an apron with a picture on it. An apple."

"You're right! I did! My sister gave it to me for a Christmas present. Fancy you remembering that!"

"I'd never seen an apron with a picture on it before."

"Must be ten years ago. No, eleven. You can't have been more than seven or eight."

"It's twelve years. More. I was six," Philip said.

"That was before Mrs. Edmund died, then."

"Yes. She was nice. I liked her," Philip said.

"We all did. Everyone around here. Terrible it was for Mr. Peter when she died. And the baby too."

"I didn't know there was a baby."

"It only lived an hour or two, they said. They thought she was going to be all right, and then suddenly . . ." She stopped. "That's a good while ago, too. But I don't think Mr. Peter ever got over it. He wasn't the same after."

There was a silence. Nobody spoke. Bran, coming back into the shop, couldn't guess what had caused it. He saw Rosemary looking troubled, Cary frightened and angry. Philip, picking up the second carton, said to Nancy Rammage, "Thanks. And thank you for sending up the stuff yesterday."

"That's all right. We'll be seeing you again."

"I expect we'll be back a lot," Philip said.

"And I'll see to it that you get your milk in the morning."

Back in the car, Cary said, "It's like feudal, isn't it? That woman's family working for yours for generations? I suppose they were serfs or something on the estate when your ancestors were the lords of the manor."

"My ancestors weren't lords of anything. The one who built the house made his money in trade. That was only about a hundred and forty years ago," Philip said.

"Well, anyway. Her mother worked for your uncle. And for his father."

"It wasn't his father. I mean, the Mr. Edward she was talking about. If he'd been Peter's father, he'd have been my grandfather, and he wasn't. He was Peter's uncle. My grandfather's brother."

"And Mr. Peter was your uncle. Why didn't they leave the house to their own children." Cary asked.

"Peter didn't have any. You heard."

Rosemary felt Cary shrug impatiently. She said, "Some of them must have, or you wouldn't be here now."

"My uncle didn't. If my father had been alive it'd have gone to him," Philip said.

There was a gap in the conversation. Rosemary thought again, as she'd thought the day before, "Why can't we talk about people dying in an ordinary way?" She knew that Philip couldn't even remember his own father—he'd been brought up by a stepfather he liked, and there were two smaller stepbrothers. Philip couldn't be feeling grief for someone he'd never known. There was no reason why they shouldn't talk about him as naturally as if he were still alive. Or had died a hundred years ago. But none of them apparently had the courage to break the taboo, and it was Bran who said next, "Would you want to live there?"

"I don't know. I . . ."

"Oh, but it's beautiful! I would!" Cary said.

"What would you do? It's miles from anywhere," Bran said.

"I don't know. Make it even more beautiful, like one of those houses you can go and visit on Sundays. Though of course it's perfect already," Cary said, anxious not to seem to criticize Philip's possession in any way.

"Plan for a perfectly useless life," Bran murmured. If Cary heard, she took no notice. "Did you really remember that woman? Or were you pretending?" she asked Philip, and Bran answered for him. "Of course he did. You ought to know by now. Philip's like George Washington. He cannot tell a lie."

"It was a big red-and-yellow apple. It remained me of the one in *Snow White and the Seven* . . ."

"The red half had poison in it and the yellow didn't. I always wondered how the stepmother managed it," Rosemary said.

"Magic," Bran said in a matter-of-fact voice.

"No, but really. Could you do it? Scientifically?" Rosemary asked.

"You think science is the same as magic," Bran said.

"I don't!"

"Yes, you do. The other day you asked me whether a vacuum was light or dark. You don't know anything about science, so you like to pretend it's magic. Or a holy sort of mystery. You think anyone could do anything. . . ."

"If you'd lived a hundred years ago . . ." Philip began.

"I know! And someone had told you you'd be able to see what was happening in a studio fifteen hundred miles away . . . Don't give me that! Rosemary doesn't want to understand. She'd rather believe it's all gobbledy-gook."

"I wouldn't! It's just I haven't a scientific sort of mind. . . ."

"You don't know what you mean by a scientific mind. It's like the tin opener. . . ."

"It isn't! You've got a scientific mind," Rosemary said.

"What tin opener?" Philip asked. But no one answered. Bran drove faster when he was cross. The car cut corners and threw spiked darts of muddy water from the rainpools in the ruts of the road. It was cold and the rain was now coming down in earnest, in steady, steel-gray rods, sharp as needles. No one spoke much while they unpacked their supplies in the comfort of the warm kitchen. During a scrappy lunch, Cary kept up a desultory conversation with Philip. Rosemary was silent. Bran felt sorry he'd been short with her.

After the meal was over, he went out to put the car away in the disused coach house which did for a garage. When he came back Rosemary was alone in the kitchen, standing at the window and looking out at the water running across the cobbled yard. He thought her back looked dejected. She didn't turn around. He came up to stand behind her.

"Sorry I was fierce."

She did turn then. "It's all right."

"Sure?"

"Sure. And you're right. I am stupid about . . ."

"Tin openers?"

They laughed.

"Where're the others?"

"Cary said she was tired. She wanted a siesta."

"I suppose she dragged Philip off to bed with her too?"

"Not exactly dragged. But he went off somewhere. I don't know where to."

"What about you? You were yawning your head off this morning. Didn't you sleep last night?"

"Yes, I did. Only it didn't feel like it this morning."

"Cheese for supper," Bran said. Seeing her look of complete mystification, he laughed. "Don't you know? Cheese for supper's meant to give you bad dreams."

"But I didn't dream. Not at all. P'raps . . . No. That's silly."

"What's silly?"

"I like dreaming. Generally, I do."

"Even if you don't remember it, you always dream. It's been proved. Scientifically!" He laughed again.

"I didn't feel as if I'd had any dreams, though. Just . . . sleep."

"I could think of something better than just sleep." She moved a little away from him.

"Rosey? You've got to make up your mind, you know."

She walked to the table and began folding paper bags and oblongs of brown paper as if her mind were on nothing else. She said, in a small voice, "I know."

"What are you waiting for? Is it magic again? Think a fairy godmother's going to come along and tell you whether I'm your golden boy or not?"

33

"No. It's just . . ."

"What? Come on. What is it all about? What are you frightened of? Is it me?"

"No."

"Sex, then?"

Rosemary said with difficulty, "I suppose I could be." She expected that this would provoke Bran's scorn, but he said, gently, "That's all right. So's everyone. Most people, anyway."

"I thought . . . I thought everyone thought it was wonderful."

"The first time? Of course they don't. Most people do it because they think everyone else is doing it. I don't mean they don't want to, but they're frightened, too. And whatever people tell you, you don't really know what it's like. Not until you've done it yourself."

Rosemary found that without noticing it, she was twisting a short length of twine around and around the fourth finger of her left hand. Without looking at Bran she asked, "You have. Have you?"

"Yes."

"What was . . . Didn't you like it?"

"I did. I was dead scared first, though."

"*You* were?"

"But I'm not now. And you don't have to be. I'd make sure it was all right for you." He came over and put an arm round her shoulders. He said, "Rosey?"

She smelled his familiar smell. She liked having his arm round her. She liked him, a lot. She couldn't explain to herself any more than she could to him why she was so hesitant about going to bed with him. She said, "Were you really scared? That first time?"

"I told you. Everyone is. Well, most people."

"I thought . . ."

"I know! You thought it was like in those rotten stories you read. Where the bloke and the girl look into each other's eyes and sink down on the grass and then afterwards he says, 'How'd you feel?' and she says, 'Darling, I didn't know it could be like this.' And he says, 'It'll be even better next time. I promise.' "

Rosemary laughed.

"That's exactly what they say. How did you know?"

"I've read enough sloshy stuff in my time. The only bit that's right about that is that it generally is better next time. That's why you'd be clever if you get your first go over with me, so you'll be ready for Prince Charming when he comes along. Just think how grateful you ought to be to me! And him, too."

"You wouldn't expect me to be . . . good at it?"

"You'd learn. Practice makes perfect."

"I'm frightened I won't . . . that I won't do the right things."

"Love, everyone thinks that at first, but you don't see the race exactly dying out, do you?"

"Suppose I got pregnant?"

"Aren't you on the Pill?"

Rosemary hesitated and this time it was Bran who laughed. "You are, aren't you? So what did you expect, coming here with me?"

"I thought we might. Only . . ."

"What?"

"Don't be angry, Bran. It's just . . . somehow being here with Cary and Philip . . . and the house. It's not like I thought. I feel . . . as if I don't belong here. I feel . . ." But she couldn't explain how she felt. Crowded yet lonely. Wanting Bran to make love to her and yet not wanting Cary and Philip to know. Especially Cary. Feeling watched. Feeling lost, unsure of her ground. She said, "I hadn't realized it was going to be like this. I mean, with us knowing whenever Cary and Philip are together and them knowing about us."

"Nothing to know yet," Bran said.

"I wish we hadn't come here with them."

"Should we leave them to it? Go away, just us two?"

"They couldn't stay here without the car. Besides . . ."

Bran knew what she meant. He knew that Philip had asked them to come not only because they were all friends. He'd said, half joking, "Of course it's the car I'm interested in." It wasn't just the car, but it wasn't Bran for himself, either. Philip had been interested in Rosemary earlier in the year, and Bran suspected that when she'd made it clear that there was nothing doing and Cary had very much come on the scene, she'd prompted Philip to ask Bran to keep Rosemary company. Not that he objected, it suited him fine. But it meant that Rosemary was being paired off with him more definitely than she'd probably foreseen. He mustn't rush her.

She was right. They couldn't go off and leave the others here stranded, without any means of transport.

She was right too, though he wouldn't admit it to her, about the house. It did feel strange. He'd thought it was because he wasn't used to this sort of living. This was a gentleman's house; a house in which one set of men and women had sat and slept and eaten and done nothing in return, while another set worked hard to keep them fed and warmed and comfortable. Bran was used to a different way of life. He'd been born and brought up in a farmhouse with sagging ceilings and creaking wooden stairs, where everyone worked almost as soon as they were walking. In the lambing season both his dad and his mum might be up for nights in a row, and at it all day too. He couldn't remember the time when he hadn't been put to helping. Collecting the eggs—he'd been doing that when he was five; then herding the sheep or the cattle from one field to another, and later driving the old tractor and feeling something like a man at the ripe age of eleven. No wonder if he felt out of place here. He was surprised, though, that Rosemary shouldn't be at ease. She came from a different social class from his; there'd been others in her family who'd been to college, and though they didn't have servants—Bran didn't know anyone who did nowadays—he guessed that the house she lived in was more like this one of Philip's than like the farm. He wondered, briefly, if he'd ever see her house, meet her mum and dad, and if so what they'd make of him, whether they'd accept him for what he was himself, or look down on him because he and his family were working class. But it wasn't Bran's way to spend time on speculating about the future. He switched back to the present and said, "No, you're right. We can't very well go."

"Perhaps it'll be better when the other two get here," Rosemary said.

"Depends what this Jamie's like."

"I saw him once. He came for the day to see Philip."

"What's he like, then?"

"He's very good-looking. But . . . I don't really know. I thought he was a bit showing off. But it might just have been that he was embarrassed."

"Doesn't sound as if he's going to be much of a help," Bran said.

"I wish the sister wasn't coming with him."

Bran said, "We'll have to see," He squeezed Rosemary's shoulders, put a gentle hand on her breast, took it away, and said, "It's all right. Let it ride. Wait till you feel easier here."

In her gratitude for his forebearance, Rosemary wanted to say, "I'll come to your room tonight." But prevented herself. She must feel right about it, or it wouldn't work for either of them. They sat opposite each other at the kitchen table, Bran immersed in the physiology of the kidney, Rosemary reading Blake's *Songs of Innocence* with puzzled pleasure. Half the time she didn't understand him, but the words made lovely patterns in her mind and occasional phrases sounded echoes deep down somewhere inside where she didn't think, only felt. From time to time she looked across at Bran, who was frowning at his book and tormenting his already wild hair into tufted peaks. Sometimes, one of them would catch the other's eye and smile. They sat there silently until it was near suppertime, when Cary appeared, dazzling in a trouser suit that emphasized her slenderness and her brilliant coloring. She announced that tonight she was going to cook the meal and that she must have the whole of the kitchen table for its preparation. Two and a half hours later, she served it; it tasted and looked exquisite, every detail attended to, like an illustration out of a color supplement. Late as it was, Philip didn't make an appearance until they had halfway demolished the first course, when he came in, soaked and cold from a walk he'd taken up the valley. In spite of the food, it was an uncomfortable supper. Cary alternated between pride in her achievement and annoyance that she could get nothing out of Philip beyond monosyllabic answers to her leading questions. By common consent, they went to bed early. As she lay in the narrow bed, Rosemary thought of Bran and of what he'd said. She must think about it more tomorrow. Sleep came quickly. She did not dream.

3

"What time's your friend Jamie arriving?" Cary asked suddenly in the middle of the next morning's work in the kitchen.

"Four forty this afternoon."

"Who's going to meet them?"

"I'll have to, because of the car," Bran said.

"Phil can drive," Cary said.

"Not if you'd rather I didn't," Philip said to Bran.

"I don't mind. Only it's not insured for anyone except me. Just don't run over a policeman, that's all."

"Then . . . perhaps I'd better not."

"Suit yourself."

"Do you mind going? I'd feel really bad if anything happened. . . ."

40

"You wouldn't be the only one," Bran said. He said to Rosemary, "Why don't you come too?" at the same moment as Cary said, "I'll come with you, shall I?"

There was a moment's pause. Then Bran said, "Rosemary's met Jamie. She'll recognize him."

"Why don't both of you go?" Philip asked.

"Car won't take five people if they bring a lot of gear," Bran said, and Cary said quickly, "Rosemary and I'll toss for it." She took a coin out of her jeans pocket and said to Rosemary, "Call!" as she spun it in the air.

"Heads," Rosemary said, unwillingly.

"Bad luck! It's tails." She put the coin back into her pocket, and looking across at Bran, she half closed one eye. Bran returned her stare stonily. He wasn't going to be drawn into a conspiracy with Cary. When he glanced at Rosemary she had her head down. He had the impression she was deliberately avoiding his eye. Later, when he looked up from his notes again, he thought he saw Cary's lips curved in secret satisfaction and he felt angry with himself. He'd let her rush him, and Rosey was justifiably angry. He ought to have slapped bloody Cary down. She was only using him to play against Philip—she wasn't interested in him for his own sake. Which meant, he supposed, that Philip wasn't proving as easy a prey as she'd hoped. That morning at breakfast Bran had thought that Philip looked tired. Shagged out, was how he'd put it to himself. Now he wondered was it really shortage of sleep because of sex that had given him a drawn, heavy-eyed look. "I hope to God he's not going to be ill. Worst of being a medical student is that everyone thinks you know how to cure every disease under the sun, when the nearest you've got to a patient is dissecting a dogfish's nervous system," Bran thought. At least in this first year at college he was learning about human anatomy. Tricky, it was, too. He sighed, and went back to the muscle attachments of the forearm.

Bran wasn't the only person to have noticed Philip's looks. When Bran and Cary had left, towards the end of the long, gray afternoon, Rosemary saw Philip sit at the table, his head supported by his hands, not, she could have sworn, working. It was the attitude of someone worn out, or in despair. Cary? she wondered. More than once she considered speaking, then checked herself, feeling that it was none of her business, until he moved and drew a long breath that seemed to come from deep inside him. Before she knew she was going to speak, Rosemary said, "What's the matter?"

He looked up, startled.

"You sighed."

"Did I?"

"Are you very tired?"

He said, considering, "No. I don't think I'm tired. It's just I can't seem to concentrate properly."

"I know. You find your eyes have got to the bottom of the page and your mind hasn't taken in a word."

"That's it! Only I keep on thinking about other things. Crazy things."

"It happens to everyone sometimes."

"They don't think about the things I think about."

"What sort of things?"

"Crazy. I said." But he didn't enlarge on this. He didn't look back at his book, either, and Rosemary waited to see if he wanted to go on talking.

"I hope Jamie'll be all right here," Philip said presently.

Rosemary understood this to mean "I hope Jamie will fit in with my other friends." She said, "How well did you know him at school?"

"Quite well. At least I thought so, then. I've been to his house once or twice."

"You said the sister doesn't talk. What's she like?"

Philip said, "She's just a kid. She's all right, I expect. I liked the parents, though. They're really nice. Intelligent. They make you feel as if they thought you were a proper person. You know. Not just another teenage nuisance."

"Isn't Jamie like them, then?"

"It's just . . . I don't know how he and Bran will get on."

Rosemary had her doubts about this too, but seeing Philip worrying as he was apt to do over other people's feelings made her say with more confidence than she really felt, "I expect they'll be all right. Bran's not difficult, really."

Philip smiled at her. He had a friendly, attractive smile. "You really like him, don't you?"

Rosemary wished she didn't blush so easily. "Yes. He's different from most people I've known."

"Different from John Tarot?" Philip asked.

"Don't be horrible!" John Tarot was one of the lecturers at college. For most of her first term, Rosemary had thought he was the most wonderful, most intelligent, sexiest man she'd ever seen, and Philip, in whom she'd confided, had been kind and ready to console her if she'd let him for the hopelessness of her passion. The passion had worn itself out as she discovered that her idol cultivated first-year worshippers and wasn't above using their admiration to undermine the confidence of his plain, hard-working wife. It had been Philip she'd gone to then for comfort, and though he hadn't been able to offer much, he'd at least listened, and lent her an enormous colored handkerchief to cry into, and had never said, "I told you so." Kind Philip. She felt very warm towards him.

"Bran's all right," Philip said.

They smiled at each other. Rosemary wished she could bring herself to say, "So's Cary." But she couldn't. Philip's eyes turned back to his book again, and Rosemary, reassured, went back to bloody Johnson. Why couldn't he have left the poets alone?

In the car, Bran and Cary hadn't spoken very much more than Philip and Rosemary in the kitchen. This was not Cary's fault. She'd begun, the moment they'd left the house. "Phil's such a fusser. I'm sure it won't take half an hour to get to the station. He's a terrible old maid in some ways, isn't he?"

"Never noticed it," Bran said.

"About time, he is. He thinks being a little bit late is an absolute crime."

Bran said nothing.

"Of course I didn't mind leaving a bit early. Gives us more time together."

No answer.

"I haven't seen you properly since we got here, Bran. Have I?"

"I haven't been hiding."

"But we've never had time to really talk."

"What about?"

"I don't know. Nothing special. Just about us. I don't feel I really know what you're like at all."

Bran said, "No," deadpan. Cary tried again.

"You guessed, didn't you? About it not being tails when I said it was. When I tossed for who was coming with you this afternoon?"

"You were lying," Bran said.

"You can't call that a lie! Anyway, I only did it so that I could come with you."

"I'd asked Rosemary."

"Do you think Rosemary's pretty?" Cary asked.

Bran said, "You'd better not talk to me while I'm driving in this rain. You don't want me to have an accident."

Cary said, "I didn't know I was so distracting." But she sounded less confident than the words implied, and she hardly spoke for the rest of the way to the station.

They were early. They'd been standing for nearly five minutes under the slight shelter of the old-fashioned wooden roof before they heard the panting of the engine, and saw the yellow face of the diesel rounding the curve.

The train pulled up, doors flew open, people got out. A group of schoolchildren, an elderly couple, two women with umbrellas carrying loaded shopping bags. A tall young man with a suitcase, who looked up and down the platform and didn't turn to help the girl who followed him. The doors banged shut, the station guard blew his whistle, and the train moved off. "That must be Jamie," Cary said, as if, Bran thought, this wasn't blindingly obvious. She moved off to meet him. Bran followed more slowly.

When he'd come up to the group, Cary was saying, in a soft, breathless voice, "You must be Jamie. I'm Cary Wilkinson. I'm at college with Philip. This is Bran." She did it very prettily, but Bran noticed that having said, "Hi!" to the girl, she concentrated her attention on the brother. She was saying now, "I know you've visited Phil at college, but I don't think we met." Jamie said, "No, we didn't. I wouldn't have forgotten," and Cary, all eyes on his face, breathed, "Nor would I."

The kid sister, Bran noticed, stood still, waiting. As far as Cary and Jamie were concerned, Bran thought, she might have waited forever. He said, "I'll take your case, shall I?" and she said, "Thank you." Philip was right about her not speaking. The other two were at it, playing up to each other like crazy, while Bran stowed the two cases in the boot. When he came back to the driver's seat, he found that Cary had settled herself in the backseat and, with a half-sketched gesture, invited Jamie to share it with her. The kid sister silently got in beside Bran.

After a minute or two, he felt sorry enough for her, thinking she probably knew she was here on sufferance and might anyway feel awkward at being so much the youngest, to say, "Ever been to this part of the country before?"

"No."

"None of the rest of us have, either. Only Philip. Unless your brother knows it."

"No, he doesn't."

"Where do you come from? What part of the world?"

"We've been living in London," the girl said.

"You at school there?"

"Yes."

After a minute's pause, Bran said, "Cary introduced us to you, but I don't know your name."

"I'm Veryan," she said.

Funny name, Bran thought, but didn't say. He couldn't think of any other topic of conversation and the kid didn't seem to want to talk, so he gave up trying and listened instead with scornful amusement to Cary doing her thing with Jamie. "Did you really?" he heard her say, and "Brilliant! How ever did you think of that?"

The car turned into the drive. Into the darkness of the overhanging branches and the crowding shrubs. He felt the girl beside him shrink into herself as if the black leafy fingers might reach in through the car windows to touch her. As they came out into the space in front of the house, he heard her give something between a gasp and an exclamation. He said, "Yes, that's how we all felt when we saw it. Fancy all that belonging to old Philip!"

The house stood white and elegant against the gray of the surrounding hillside and the black, sodden trees. In spite of its size it managed to appear light, delicate. Something to do with its proportions, Bran supposed. Those slender pillars were really as tough as steel girders, and the narrow windows were separated by just enough stuccoed stone to give the appearance of fragility. A superb piece of architectural engineering, to build a substantial great mansion like this and to make it look as delicate as lace.

The girl shivered again. Bran said, "Get indoors quick and warm up quick. Rosemary'll make us a pot of tea." He took the shallow steps at a leap, opened the door and called, "Hi! We're back!" deliberately loud and rough, as if he could shock the house out of its genteel propriety.

Rosemary came out onto the steps. She saw Cary uncoiling from the backseat, followed by Jamie, as good-looking and as carefully dressed as she remembered. No kid sister, then, after all? Then she saw her, standing on the farther side of the car. A small, unremarkable girl, with none of Jamie's impressiveness. Straight, mousey hair, cut shoulder length and square above the eyebrows; a belted raincoat; jeans. A typical schoolgirl, probably about fourteen. Cary didn't wait to bring her in—she'd made straight for the warmth of the kitchen, leaving the boys to carry the cases and the girl to find her own way in. In spite of her resolve not to be pushed into doing a mothering act, Rosemary came down the steps and said to the girl, "Why don't you come in? It's cold out here."

The girl followed her up to the door. Rosemary, turning to make sure that she was close behind, found herself looking into the girl's eyes. Why should that be a shock? A surprise? She'd never seen eyes like that before. Without meaning to, she said, "You've got deep-water eyes!" Then, astonished at herself, she said, "I'm sorry."

The girl's eyes regarded her steadily. The pupils were huge black holes in the honey-brown iris, flecked with colors as the water of a stream is flecked with the colors reflected from the sky, the green of leaves, and the gold of catkins in spring.

Rosemary said again, "I'm sorry."

"It's all right. Jamie says they're gooseberry eyes."

"But gooseberries . . . No. That's not right."

"My father used to say treacle." The girl stepped into the hall and looked around.

"It's beautiful, don't you think?" Rosemary said.

"I suppose it is."

"I'm afraid I don't know your name. I'm Rosemary and that's Philip." He had just appeared coming from the passage which led to the kitchen.

"I know Philip."

"Yes, of course. I . . ."

Philip came up to them. "Hullo, Veryan. I'm glad you could come."

She said, "Hullo," in a small voice, not looking at him. Rosemary thought, "She doesn't like him. Poor kid." Then, remembering her resolve, she said in what, too late, she heard as her schoolma'am voice, "Do you want to go upstairs first, or would you like to have a cup of tea in the kitchen?"

"Tea, please."

Cary was already in the kitchen, huddled over the Rayburn, complaining of the cold. Rosemary filled the white porcelain teapot which suited the house, but didn't somehow seem as comfortable as an old brown earthenware pot would have been. Before she'd poured all the mugs, Philip and Jamie had come in, followed almost immediately by Bran.

"You've met Rosemary," Philip said to Jamie.

"Yes. Lovely to see you again," Jamie said, charm very much in evidence. Rosemary muttered what she hoped sounded more appreciative than she felt. She'd noticed Jamie's eyes sliding away from her towards Cary even while he was greeting her. She wondered if the sister was the same, all show and nothing beyond. She certainly wasn't putting on any sort of show at the moment; she was sitting drinking her tea, silent while the rest of them talked. Rosemary thought again, "Poor kid, it's going to be horribly lonely for her here. It was stupid of Jamie to bring her. She ought to be with kids of her own age." She tried to remember what she'd been like at fourteen. Only four years ago, but it seemed like another life. Bran had told her once that the first four weeks of a baby's life in the womb were the weeks of the fastest growth in the whole of the rest of its lifetime. But those four years between fourteen and eighteen had seen the greatest change Rosemary could remember in her own inside life. What had she thought about when she was this kid's age? Netball, best friends—Eleanor who had turned out to be such a prig—six months of pining for a pony, an agonized passion for a pop singer whom she'd never so much as seen in real life, floods of tears because Miss Thorne said her poem wasn't good enough for the school magazine. Endless fights with Mum about her hair, her clothes, her shoes, her homework. Reading Lady Chatterley behind the school sheds in break and suddenly realizing what Miss Davies' incomprehensible sex talks had been about. Wearing perfume for the first time, running away dead scared when a passing motorist had tried to pick her up. Taking her ancient, lopsided, bald monkey to bed with her, knowing it was babyish, promising herself each night that this was for the very last time, and then, the next night, being unable to resist the comforting feel of Pongo in her arms. She'd felt at the same time enormously old and worldly wise, and inexperienced and frightened. An uncomfortable age. "I'm glad I'll never be fourteen again," Rosemary thought.

Bran toasted bread and spread it with butter. "Gourmet's delight," he said, offering it to the others. Cary accepted—"What a wonderful idea, I haven't eaten hot buttered toast for years,"—Philip and Jamie first refused, then succumbed. Veryan accepted her share and ate it neatly and without comment. Rosemary, when Bran turned to her, shook her head.

"Come on. Everyone else is, even Philip."

"I oughtn't to."

"Toast isn't a sin," Bran said, leaning slightly on the word Toast. Rosemary felt herself color.

"It's fattening," she said.

"Then it'll make up for all the energy you're putting into hating every word you read."

"I don't!"

"A lot of it, you do. You should have seen yourself this morning, longing to throw the book out of the window or into the fire. If we'd had one."

"It was Carlyle," Rosemary said.

"He's an old windbag. But it's rhetoric. Meant to be declaimed out loud," Bran said.

"You've read him?" Rosemary said, surprised.

"In my misspent youth," Bran said.

"You're extraordinary. Did you know? A medical student and you read Carlyle! I bet you've read more literature than all of us put together," Cary said.

"I'm not competing," Bran said.

"Cary's right, it is amazing. When do you have time to read outside your subject?" That was Jamie.

"Here's your share of the delights of the flesh," Bran said, putting a half slice of toast in front of Rosemary instead of answering. She ate it, thinking that Cary was right, Bran was extraordinary, not only because he'd read so much, but more because he didn't show off about his knowledge.

"Any more tea in that pot? Wake up! You can't go to sleep yet," Bran said, handing her his mug.

"Which reminds me. Shall I show you your rooms?" Cary said, standing up. She left the room without giving any of the others a chance to answer. Jamie looked around the table, murmured, "Better go and see," and followed her. Veryan got up and disappeared after them.

"Quite the lady of the house," Bran said. Philip got up, went towards the door, and then hesitated.

"Why don't you go too? It is your house, not hers," Bran said. Philip went, and as the door shut behind him, Bran exploded.

"Why doesn't he stand up to her? Bloody, interfering little bitch!"

"He does sometimes," Rosemary said.

"Not since we've been here, he hasn't. He just lies down and lets her walk all over him."

"Well. You let her come with you this afternoon."

"That's true."

"Why did you?"

"Did you mind?"

"I minded you letting her. Not so much the not coming to the station. Why did you?"

"It didn't seem worth making a song and dance about."

"Perhaps that's how Philip feels."

"It'll serve him right if he finds himself committed to sharing the four-poster with Cary for the rest of the fortnight," Bran said.

"You really think she will?"

"Well, she won't be putting you in with me without asking, more's the pity. And I doubt if she's going to invite me to her royal bed. And it would be a bit quick to have Jamie in with her this first day. Though I somehow don't think she's going to rule him right out by putting him in with me. So she's either got to make a pair of you and the kid, or she's going to gobble old Philip up. My guess is for that."

He was right. Cary came back into the kitchen five

minutes later and said, "I've put Jamie into the room next to ours, and his sister's along at the top of the stairs next to the yellow bathroom. I hope that's all right with everyone? That means that neither of you two has to move."

"All done for our benefit?" Bran asked.

"It seemed the best way."

The best for Cary, Bran thought. She was looking pleased with herself. She'd nailed Philip, almost certainly without asking him. Now if he wanted to move out, he'd have to take active steps to do it. Which meant that, however much he didn't want to, he'd probably stay. Like judo, Bran thought—Cary had used his hesitation and inertia to bring him down. And if she was underneath physically, like Venus, she was certainly on top emotionally and mentally.

Bran raised an eyebrow at Rosemary when Cary wasn't looking and she grimaced back.

At least, he thought, Cary hadn't put either of them to share with anyone else. She hadn't absolutely buggered him and Rosey up. Not yet.

4

It was Rosemary's turn to cook supper.

"Don't get so het up," Bran said, seeing her frown with anxiety as she broke eggs into a pudding basin.

"I've never cooked on a Rayburn before. Suppose I make a mess of it and there's nothing for anyone to eat?"

"You won't. But if you did, there's always bread and cheese. Anyway, the worst you can do to scrambled eggs is to make them watery. Don't put any milk in, and then if they do go wrong they'll turn into an omelette. That's all."

"I might burn them."

"Hopeful, aren't you?"

She didn't burn the eggs but, painfully conscious of the others sitting around waiting to eat, and observing her, she did burn the toast on which the scrambled eggs were to be served. Bran was scraping black crumbs into the bin, and the eggs were just taking on that clumped, shiny look which means that they're ready, when Philip said, "Where's Veryan?"

No one answered at first. Then Jamie said, "She was in her room, unpacking."

"That was ages ago. And it's cold upstairs," Philip said. He opened the kitchen door and went out into the hall. He called, "Ver-y-an!" As he came back into the room, he said, "She must be frozen."

"She might have gone for a walk," Jamie said.

"In the dark?" Bran said. He was angry with all of them, including himself. He remembered what it was like to be the youngest, to be taken along because there was no one to leave him with. He ought to have thought about the kid before this, instead of sitting comfortably in the warm kitchen, looking at Rosemary and wondering what his next, best tactic would be. But he'd forgotten Veryan. They all had. Rosey with her cooking, he with Rosey, Jamie and Cary, eyeing each other, carrying on half-whispered, laughing conversations. And Philip? Whatever he'd been thinking about as he sat there with a book in front of him, it hadn't been Veryan, that was clear.

She came down apparently as composed as before, and she didn't look as chilled as Bran had expected. She was wearing an immense dark blue fisherman's sweater, several sizes too large. She had rolled the sleeves up above her wrists but the shoulders sagged over the upper part of her arms and the bottom of it came down to just above her knees. Bran's "What a smashing sweater!" came at the same time as Jamie's exclamation, "That's Dad's jersey!"

Veryan didn't answer Jamie. To Bran she said, "It's warm."

"Why didn't you come down when you'd finished unpacking?" Jamie said next.

"I thought you'd all be working."

"Weren't you cold upstairs?" Philip asked.

"Not very."

Cary and James did most of the talking during supper. Each, Bran thought, out to impress the other. Cary's way was to exert charm indiscriminately all around. The house was fantastic, Rosemary's cooking was delicious, Bran was so clever at driving. Her eyes said that Jamie was the best-looking man she'd ever met. Jamie agreed with everything she said. The house was great, the meal was great, it was great to be there. He'd been absolutely delighted when he'd heard the news that old Philip had been left a place in the country. He'd hoped he might be invited there someday, but of course he hadn't realized what a miracle of a place it was. He looked at Cary as he said it, and made it clear that the house wasn't the only unexpected miracle he'd encountered here.

"You and Phil were at school together, weren't you?"

"That's right. The old school tie. Do you ever go back to see them all again?" Jamie asked Philip.

"No."

"I dropped in at the end of the Michaelmas term just to see how they were all getting on," Jamie said.

"The what term?" Bran asked.

"Michaelmas. That's what we call it at Oxbridge. Autumn, then. Silly, really, these names. Quite out of date."

"No, I think it's pretty. Sort of traditional. I wish we had more old traditions," Cary said.

"You wouldn't if you had to live with them. Imagine having to dress up in evening dress to take your exams! Even the girls do."

"I wouldn't mind that," Cary said.

"How'd you like to be in a one-sex college, then?"

"All girls?"

"Or all men. I mean . . . in this day and age! It's ridiculous!"

"Why did you go there if you think it's all stupid?" Bran asked.

"Well . . . you know. It's been a sort of family tradition. My father was at the college, and one of my grandfathers. So it seemed sort of the right thing to go there."

"I'd have given anything to go to Oxbridge," Cary said.

"Why didn't you?"

"No one at my school thought I'd have a chance of getting in."

"Of course you'd have got in. I'm sure you're cleverer than most of the dimwits I see around," Jamie said.

"I'm sure I'm not. Everyone knows you have to be brilliant to get into Oxbridge," Cary said.

Rosemary looked at Philip. Didn't he mind Cary's making up to Jamie? But Philip seemed not to have noticed what was going on. He had finished eating, and he was sitting at the table, his eyes unfocused, his mind a long way away from anything there. She had a sudden lurch of the heart, as if Philip's absentmindedness had been a threat. But that was silly. If Philip didn't care how much Cary and Jamie flirted, so much the better. She didn't want Philip as a boyfriend herself, but she didn't like him being tied up with Cary. Not being dog in the manger, but because Cary was a taker, a grabber. Philip wasn't. He was generous, vulnerable, someone who could easily get hurt.

She looked round the table and saw that Veryan's extraordinary eyes were also fixed on Philip. She was sitting as motionless as he was, but while he was lost in some process of internal cogitation, Veryan appeared to Rosemary to be completely aware of her surroundings; or, rather, of the object of her attention. Like a cat watching a mousehole. No, that wasn't right. She wasn't waiting to pounce. More like a mother cat watching her kittens from a little distance; apparently relaxed, but observing every move. Why? What was she waiting for? Or if she wasn't waiting, what did she find in Philip to engross so much attention?

Because she herself felt uncomfortable, Rosemary said, across the table, "Philip!"

The others stopped talking and looked at her, but Philip didn't move.

"Philip!" Louder.

He started and his eyes focused on her.

"What?"

"You were miles away. I just wanted to wake you up."

"I wasn't asleep."

"What were you thinking about?" Cary asked.

"Nothing. I don't know."

Next time Rosemary looked towards Veryan, she was looking down at her plate.

After supper Bran suggested cards. That would mean that the kid would have to be included. He was amused to notice that she played without giving anything away. Even while the others were exclaiming and shouting at Racing Demon, she hardly spoke, and when they'd changed to Slippery Ann, her remarkable ability to keep a composed face stood her in good stead. Impossible to guess whether she held good cards or bad. "Do you play poker?" he asked her, when she'd beaten them all hands down by collecting the whole bag of forfeits without letting any of them guess what she was aiming at.

She did smile at him then. "Sometimes I do."

"Poker? You don't," Jamie said.

"Dad and I played sometimes with Sammy."

"I didn't know." He sounded affronted.

"I bet you always won," Bran said.

"I didn't always. Why?"

"You've got the perfect poker face."

He'd been interested too to observe how the others played. Cary was good; she played to win, she concentrated, and she had an excellent memory. Jamie was poor; he was a conversational player, whose mistakes were the direct result of his lack of attention. Rosemary played as she did everything, carefully, but without enough confidence for brilliance. Philip played erratically; in the first few games he'd seemed as eager as Cary and with nearly as good a card sense, but after a time he apparently lost interest, and presently excused himself and left the table. Bran looked at him, sitting apart from the rest of them with a book, and thought, "Poor old Philip!" and then wondered why. Wondered what he found pitiable about Philip. Here he was, sitting in a house which he owned, which must be worth more than Bran or any of his family were likely to earn in a lifetime. He had Cary, one of the most attractive girls on the campus, ready to take him to bed. But in spite of all this, Bran knew that he'd never be envious of Philip. Philip was one of those people who would always see too many sides of every question, would be an easy prey to self-doubt. He lacked the emotional energy which made Bran certain of what he meant to do and which would give him no peace until he had achieved it. Which reminded him of what he wanted here and now. Somehow or other he had to talk to Rosemary alone. And soon.

He said to her abruptly, "Come out and look at the stars."

She looked startled. "Are there any?"

"That's what we'll find out."

She followed him out into the hall. He picked up her coat and held it out to her. "Put it on; it'll be cold." He threw his own around his shoulders, opened the front door, and stepped into the darkness outside.

As soon as his eyes had got used to it, he saw. There were stars. Millions of them. Unbelievable millions of light years away, they pierced the black velvet with throbbing pinpricks of brilliance. Bran stood with his face turned up towards the sight. Rosemary came and stood beside him.

"You see? There they are."

"What's that big bright one? Over there, nearly behind the hill."

"Probably a planet if it's that bright."

"I wish I knew about stars," Rosemary said.

"How to tell your fortune by them?"

"No. Which one's which. The constellations. That sort of thing. All I know's the Bear."

"I was all ready to tell you what the future holds for you." He put an arm round her and pulled her closer.

"Go on, then. Tell me." She gave a little shiver.

"Cold?"

"No."

"There's a likely lad wants to sleep with you, and you're going to agree."

She was silent. Bran took heart from the fact that she didn't draw away. He touched her cheek with his lips, then kissed her on the mouth.

"Rosey? You want me too."

She said, "Do I?" in a small voice.

"Don't you know you do, you twit?"

"I feel . . . I suppose that's what it is."

"It's smashing old sex, love, rearing its hideous head. The sooner you learn to recognize it, the better."

"All right," Rosemary said.

"That's my girl." He kissed her again, more thoroughly.

"Don't pull away," he said.

"I just want to say, where?"

"Pity it's so cold out here. That's what would be best."

Rosemary said, "Out of doors?" in a voice that made him laugh.

"Now you're talking like my great auntie. She thought that nothing sinful ever took place except in bed, after ten o'clock at night and the lights off."

"But suppose someone saw you?"

"You find a nice safe place where no one'd think of looking. All right, love. I said it was too cold. So it's got to be either your room or mine. Shall I come knocking on your door, or will you come to mine?" He felt his excitement rising—he'd have liked to make love to her then and there, but he knew he had to be patient. She was still scared.

"My room's farther away from the others."

"I'll wait till everyone's finished in the bathroom."

"Yes, *please.*"

"It's nothing so dreadful we'll be doing, Rosey."

"I just don't want the others to know. Not Cary, anyhow."

"Cary's going to be thinking about other things than us tonight," Bran said.

He felt Rosemary shiver again. "Come on, we'd best be getting back." He wanted to go in and pack the lot of them off to bed, quickly. He wanted the moment to arrive when he'd heard the plug being pulled for the last time, when he'd heard the last room door shut, when he could tap on Rosemary's door and let himself in. He felt that his hands knew already that her body's skin would be warm and silky like the skin of her cheeks and neck. He felt he knew what she'd look like naked; she'd say she was fat, no doubt, but Bran knew she'd be perfect for him, breasts, funny little sticking-out bum, and soft deep thighs. She'd be lovely. He could hardly wait. But he must; he'd got to go slowly, make sure she enjoyed herself this first time. Ordinarily he didn't go for virgins—he liked a bit of cooperation. But Rosey was different. He wanted more than for both of them to have a good time. What? Bran didn't know. He wondered, with a rueful dismay mixed with self-mockery, if perhaps he was in love.

5

"Rosey?"

"Mmm."

"Was it all right for you?"

"Some of it was."

"The beginning?"

"Yes."

It hadn't happened to Bran for ages, the failure at the crucial moment. He couldn't understand it.

"It wasn't right for you either," Rosemary said.

"No."

"I'm sorry. Was it because . . . ? Was it my fault?"

To his astonishment, Bran found himself more anxious to reassure her than to blame anything or anyone for his disappointment. He said, "Nothing to do with

65

you. It happens sometimes."

"Has it to you? With other girls?"

"Of course." And he'd minded more then, even though he'd so much wanted to succeed with Rosey. He'd felt, with Jill, not just disappointed but ashamed. Sour. He'd never tried with her again. Now he felt sad, but not angry, not wretched. He edged an arm underneath Rosemary's shoulders so that he could hold her against him, wrapped around by both arms.

"How's that?"

"That's nice." She laughed suddenly.

"What are you laughing at?"

"You haven't said it."

"Said what?"

She quoted. " 'It'll be even better next time.' "

"You take the words out of me mouth."

The single bed rocked with their stifled laughter. Bran remembered something his dad had said a long time ago. Five years perhaps. He hadn't understood it at the time, had thought it showed that his dad didn't know what sex was all about, or was past it. He'd said, "When it comes to marrying, son, pick a girl you can talk to in bed." The young Bran had said, "Talk to?" and his dad had said, "I'm not saying she's got to talk because there's nothing else she'll do. You're not likely to make a mistake like that. Too much of me in you. I'm just telling you, you'll need more than four legs in the bed. If that's all you go for, you'll make a big mistake." Then, seeing Bran's face, he'd laughed and said, "I don't mean now. Go ahead now and have all the girls you can get. I'm talking about later, when you're pick-

66

ing one for keeps." The young Bran had wanted to ask, but didn't like to, if his dad and his mum talked in bed. Then he'd supposed that probably that was all they did do there. He knew better now. He'd been twelve years the youngest—his mum had been forty-five when she'd had him, a late and much-loved mistake. Of course they'd talked, and they'd loved too. They'd certainly laughed, as he and Rosey were laughing now. He hugged her even closer and heard her sigh.

"Am I holding you too tight?"

"I like it."

"Go to sleep."

"I'd like to. Only . . ."

"I'll be sure and get myself back into my room before anyone's about."

She settled into his arms, then. He could almost hear her shut her eyes. He said, "Cozy, Rosey?"

"Mm."

Rosemary had been asleep for minutes and Bran was just sinking into a delicious drowsiness when they were torn awake by a sudden cry. It was a scream of terror, itself terrifying by its message of panic.

"What is it?" Rosemary said, breaking away from Bran's arms and sitting up. She was trembling. Bran switched on the bedside light.

"I'll go and see," he said.

"No. Wait a minute. I'd better go first."

"Look around the door. If the coast's clear, I'll come too."

She snatched up her coat from a chair and opened

her door. There was light in the passage outside. Bran saw her mouth at him to stay where he was. He heard footsteps and Rosemary asking, "What's happened?" Then her footsteps going away. He put on the coat in which he'd come from his own room, turned out the light and looked cautiously around the door.

Outside the door of the four-poster room, Cary and Philip were standing, with Rosemary beside them. They were looking towards the farther door, from which Jamie was just emerging. Bran slipped out and joined them. He asked, "What happened?"

Cary, flushed and angry, didn't answer. Philip said, "I thought it might be Rosemary . . ." Bran had an instant impulse to ask him, "Being raped?" but held his tongue. Rosemary said, "Veryan," and ran towards the small room which, like her own, looked out to the front of the house, at the end of the corridor on the opposite side of the central stairs.

She tapped at the door, then opened it. The room was totally dark. She said, "Veryan? You all right?" and switched on the light.

Veryan was sitting upright in bed. Her eyes were swollen and her breath came in gasps. She said, "Did I call out?"

"You yelled. What happened? It sounded as if someone was murdering you."

"I dreamed. I woke up when I heard myself screaming." She managed a faint, shaky smile.

Cary's voice behind Rosemary said, "What the hell's the matter?"

68

"Veryan had a bad dream."

"You woke us all up," Cary said.

"I'm sorry."

"What made you call out like that, for Chrissake?" Jamie said, appearing behind Cary.

"I was dreaming. I didn't know I was going to wake everyone up."

"As long as you're all right. You terrified me," Bran said.

"I'm sorry."

"You don't do this at home," Jamie said, very much the older brother, reproving and feeling the need to apologize for her.

"I didn't have nightmares at home."

"She couldn't help dreaming," Rosemary said to Jamie.

"She didn't have to make such a fuss about a bad dream."

"Haven't you ever woken up from a nightmare? You don't choose." For some reason Jamie's failure to stand by his sister, his aligning himself with the rest of them, young adults, against her, made Rosemary mad. She went over to the bed, sat down on it, and put her arms around Veryan. She thought that the others, grouped in their nightclothes and coats, and Jamie's blanket, looked like the Spanish Inquisition, come to claim their victim. She said, "Why don't you all go back to bed?" And saw Bran look at her, a different look from anything she'd had from him before. She couldn't put a name to it. She didn't need to. She thought, "He knows what I've got to do. Bran!" and saw him follow the others without regret.

He shut the door behind him. Rosemary pulled away from Veryan and tucked her feet, which were cold, underneath her on the bed. She said, "Want to tell me what you dreamed?"

"No."

"It frightened you?"

"It was horrible," Veryan said.

"Don't you really ever have nightmares? I used to have lots when I was a kid. Younger than you, though."

Veryan shook her head. "No."

"Don't you dream, then?"

"I dream a lot. Every night," Veryan said.

"But nice dreams?"

"They're not always good. They're . . . interesting."

"What like?"

"All sorts of things. Places. Places I don't go to except when I'm dreaming."

"Real places?"

"They're real in my dreams," Veryan said. She was still sitting up in bed, but the rigidity had gone out of her. She looked very young, less than fourteen, more like a ten-year-old, with red, puffy eyes, and hair sticking out around her face. She wore a blue-and-white-striped pajama top, as much too large for her as the fisherman's jersey had been.

"Will you be able to go to sleep again, do you think?" Rosemary asked.

"I expect I will."

"Would you like something hot to drink? I could make you tea. Only it might keep you awake. I don't know if there's anything else. Like cocoa . . ."

"I don't want anything. Thank you."

"Well . . ."

"You're cold. You can go back to bed. I'll be all right," Veryan said.

"I'll stay if you're still frightend."

"I don't think I am, now."

"If you want to, you can come and wake me up if you get frightened again. I'm in the room like yours, only the other side of the stairs." She'd have to warn Bran that he must spend the rest of the night in his own room. She found that she was sorry. Going to sleep in his arms had been good. Better than she'd expected.

"I think I'll be all right," Veryan said. She lay down in the bed, looking at Rosemary with those large honey-colored eyes.

"Sure?"

"You can't ever be sure," Veryan said.

At the door, Rosemary said, "Shall I turn out the light, then?"

"Yes, please."

In the darkness, Rosemary said, "Sleep well."

"I'm sorry if I frightened you."

"That's all right. Come and find me if you want me."

She turned out the lights in the passages as she went back towards her own room. As she came to Bran's door, it opened and he looked out.

"She all right?"

71

"I think so. I asked, and she said you can't ever be sure."

"That's true enough." They were talking in whispers.

"I told her she could come and wake me up if she gets frightened again, Bran. So . . ."

"I see."

"I'm sorry."

"Are you? Really?"

"Really."

He gave her a quick, light kiss. "Another time. Just hope the kid doesn't make a habit of it."

Rosemary got back into her bed. There was still a faint warmth beneath the covers, left from their two bodies. The pillow, too, smelled of Bran as well as of her. She didn't go to sleep at once. She was thinking of the last hour. She wasn't a virgin any longer. In old-fashioned books girls lay and wept at this thought. Or they gave their lovers ecstatic smiles and told them it had been unbelievably wonderful. Why didn't anyone write about it how it was? Bran was right when he said you couldn't guess till you'd tried, but that was because writers didn't tell all of the truth. It was exciting and extraordinary and disappointing and, because of the way you were brought up, seemed—not exactly wrong, but secret. Like sharing a secret, giving away something you'd thought you'd never be able to tell anyone. And hearing theirs. Only Bran hadn't been able to give her his secret.

Another thing no one ever told you was that sex was funny. Not the whisper-behind-the-bicycle-shed funny, but funny in itself. Trying to get the right bits to fit into the right places when you weren't used to it. Perhaps that was why they'd laughed so much afterwards. Rosemary had never thought of that sort of laughter going with making love. She couldn't remember Lady Chatterley and Mellors laughing much. With them it was all very serious.

She'd enjoyed that laughing with Bran.

She hoped Veryan didn't come and wake her up.

She slept. Again that night, she did not dream

6

Breakfast the next morning was a protracted affair, with everyone coming down at different times. For different reasons, Bran thought, looking them over at the midmorning cup of coffee, which was breakfast for Jamie, the last to appear. Cary looked like a thundercloud, and was obviously sulking—even more obviously, sulking at Philip. Philip looked bad; blue shadows under his eyes and his forehead puckered in a frown. Bran wondered what those two had been up to when the kid had yelled out, and what they'd been at since. Rosemary, he was relieved to see, looked her normal self, and the smile she'd given him when she came into the kitchen had complicity as well as warmth. Veryan, the cause of the disturbance, answered questions politely: Yes, she'd gone to sleep quickly, no, she hadn't had any more bad dreams, yes, she felt all right this morning. Without her saying a word out of place, her tone said that she was giving the answers expected. They bore no relation to the truth. If she'd said out loud that she intended to keep her thoughts and feelings to herself, she couldn't have made it plainer. So Bran thought.

Since six of them couldn't possibly work in the kitchen, they'd decided to try to warm up the dining room next door; it seemed a more promising proposition than the cold white-and-gold drawing room on the other side of the graceful square hall and farther from the comforting heat of the Rayburn. There was a supremely elegant fireplace in the dining room, and the fire Philip laid in it burned well, but somehow the room remained chill. They sat around, huddled in sweaters and parkas, like squatters occupying a house deserted by the gentlefolk who should have been there. No one found it easy to work. Cary yawned the morning away. Philip sat with the same pages of his book unturned, Bran could have sworn, for two hours, his face a mask of unhappiness. Rosemary shivered, piled on more cardigans, tried to read, found herself falling asleep over Chaucer's *Troilus and Criseyde*, made notes, which she'd never look at again, in an effort to keep awake. Jamie read, made comments only half under his breath, stretched, went for a stroll, came back, and went through the same performance again. Veryan sat nearly unmoving with a book in front of her. At one point Bran looked across the room and saw that her face was wet with tears. No sobs. She didn't make a sound. As he watched, she wiped her eyes with the sleeve of the much-too-big sweater she wore. She didn't look up. Bran felt as if he'd intruded. What a funny kid, he thought. He tried to see the title of the book she was reading. When he did, it came as a surprise. What, for God's sake, could the craziest kid find to cry about in *Robinson Crusoe*?

In the middle of their midday meal, the kitchen door opened and a woman came in. She was small and apologetic. "I didn't mean to interrupt you at your dinner. Just wanted to see if everything was all right."

Philip, speaking as if from a long way back, said, "Mrs. Eye?"

"That's right. Mr. Philip? I'd have known you anywhere."

"The woman down in the greengrocer's said he had the family face," Cary said. Mrs. Eye tittered as if this were a joke.

"He's Mr. Peter's nephew all right. And the rest of you? Just friends, are you?"

Rosemary half expected Cary to say that she was more than just a friend. But she nodded and smiled, like the rest of them.

"Well, I won't spoil your dinnertime. Everything all right, was it? Found everything nice and ready for you when you got here, did you?" She seemed to address this to Cary and it was Cary who said, "Yes, thank you. Everything was great. It was just as if someone had been living here only just before we arrived."

"I've always kept it nice. Whenever I was let to, that is."

There didn't seem any answer to this curious remark. Cary said, "It's a lovely house. We're all really jealous of Philip for having it."

"It's a lovely house all right. No one can say it isn't that," Mrs. Eye said.

"We were lucky that the lady in the village shop thought of sending up some food for us, too. We'd forgotten to lay any in," Bran said. Mrs. Eye's expression changed from gratification to annoyance.

"That Nancy Rammage can't ever keep her nose from sticking into other people's affairs," she said.

"We thought perhaps you'd asked her . . ."

"You just wrote me to get the house ready. You didn't say anything about laying in food."

"I forgot," Philip said.

"He's not used to housekeeping. Not yet. None of us are, really," Cary said, smiling at the little woman in the way very few people could resist. But Mrs. Eye was still put out. "What did she send you? A load of rubbish and then asked you London prices, I'll be bound."

"She'd thought of almost everything we needed that first night. We had a really good meal," Bran said. He didn't see why Nancy Rammage shouldn't get the credit she deserved. Mrs. Eye looked at him with scorn.

"She'd no right. Mr. Philip asked me to get the place ready. She wouldn't have known he was coming if I hadn't let it slip."

Obviously a village feud, Bran thought. If he had to

choose between Mrs. Eye and Nancy Rammage, he knew which he'd have to look after him. Mrs. Eye was now saying, "I'll just pop upstairs and see to the rooms. They could do with a bit of a dust and a tidy, I'm sure."

Rosemary, Cary, and Bran, for once united in feeling, began a protest. To be tidied for would be terrible. They'd all strewn things around as they were used to doing at college, where you could live for a term in your own comfortable mess without the fear that anyone would try to put it right for you. Rosemary had said, "Don't bother . . ." and Bran, "It's all right . . ." but they checked themselves. It was Philip's house—Mrs. Eye obviously felt that she was working for him. He was the one who should tell her not to. But Philip didn't. All he said was, "We're not very tidy, I'm afraid."

"That's all right. I'll put everything right in no time." She began to back out of the door.

"I'd rather you left my room," Rosemary said.

"I've never touched a thing that wasn't mine. No one can say I've ever laid a finger on what didn't belong to me," Mrs. Eye said.

"I didn't mean . . ."

"You ask Mr. Philip there. He'll tell you." She nodded her head towards Philip.

"Of course, I didn't mean that. It's just . . . I've left things lying about all over the place. . . ."

"I shan't take anything."

"I know." The only possible thing to say now seemed to be "Of course if you don't mind everything being so untidy . . ."

"I'll see to it," Mrs. Eye said, and disappeared.

"Christ!" Bran said.

"You upset her," Cary accused Rosemary.

"I just don't like being tidied for."

"None of us'll ever be able to find anything," Bran said.

"She thought you meant she wasn't honest."

"I never thought of that. I just don't like . . ."

"You said," Cary said.

"Anyway, we've only been here three days. I can't see why she wants to clean up around us now."

"She wants to keep the house looking nice."

"Not worth trying till after we've gone," Bran said.

"She's probably used to coming every day. Or nearly. Isn't she?" Cary asked Philip.

"I don't know."

"I thought you recognized her?"

"But that was ages ago. I told you, I was a kid. How the hell do I know how often she came here?"

Bran took notice of Philip's impatience. Good for him if he was getting sick of Cary's proprietorial manners.

"Was she your uncle's caretaker here?" Jamie asked.

"I said, I don't know what she was. I just remember seeing her once and my uncle telling me her name. I don't know whether it was in the house or in the village."

"That woman in the shop . . . she said her mother used to come up to the house while your aunt was alive," Cary said.

"What was your aunt like?" Rosemary asked.

"Aunt Patricia. All I remember is that she had white

hair. Like a wig. Like powder. She must have been quite young."

Overhead a door shut very softly.

"Oh, God! She's in my room," Bran said.

"That's funny!" Rosemary said.

"What's funny about that? It's a mess, I agree. But she's not going to be put off by a little thing like that."

"No. I meant it's funny she's so quiet."

They all sat silent, considering this. Listening.

"I mean. When someone's cleaning, you generally hear them. Vacuuming, or moving the furniture about," Rosemary said.

"You're right. She is quiet," Jamie said.

They listened again. Not a sound. Not the ghost of a footstep, not the whisper of a broom. Rosemary had a sudden vivid picture of Mrs. Eye upstairs. With a duster in her hand, in case anyone saw her; but not dusting. Not using the vacuum cleaner, not sweeping, not polishing. Instead, she would be looking around, searching for something, she herself probably didn't know what. Picking up books and reading their titles. Turning over papers, lecture notes, notebooks, and peering inside to see who doodled in the margins, who wrote messages to their neighbors in lectures, who drew rude pictures on blank spaces of paper. Opening drawers quickly, quietly, going through the contents. Not taking anything, not a thief, but making lists in her sharp, small mind, criticizing, envying: "That's a pretty necklace. I wouldn't mind having one like that. That's a nice petticoat, wish I'd got one as good." "What does she want with all these shoes?

Couldn't wear them in a month of Sundays." Or, worse, "What's this she's written down here? 'I don't know if I'm in love or not'? Here's something else. Looks like poetry." It was intolerable to think of Mrs. Eye's small, claw hands touching private possessions. Under a box of tissues in the top right-hand drawer were Rosemary's Pills. She was halfway through the month's supply— there'd be no doubt but that they were in use. Would she poke into the beds and see which held the impress of more than one body? Rosemary felt spied upon. It was demeaning, it was dirty.

Bran said, "Coffee for everyone?" Rosemary was sure he felt uneasy too, though he'd mind less what anyone knew about him. He wasn't as anxious as she was.

"I don't want coffee," Veryan said. She made for the door.

"Where're you going?" Jamie asked.

"Upstairs."

"You'll have to get out of your room so that that woman can get in to clean it," Jamie said.

Veryan looked at him and left without answering.

"Funny kid," Jamie said, apologizing for her.

"You think she's all right here?" Bran asked.

"Of course she's all right. Why shouldn't she be?"

Bran didn't want to give away the tears he'd seen on her face. He said, "Being so much the youngest. And not having to work like us."

"She's all right. She's always reading at home," Jamie said.

"Doesn't she ever talk?" Rosemary asked.

"Sometimes she does. She might be a bit shy, not knowing any of you. But she's all right," Jamie said again. He went over to the sink where Cary, whose turn it was, was slowly and reluctantly wiping the dishes with a mop. Jamie said in a fake cockney accent, "Allow me to assist you, ducks," and dried the cutlery as she handed it to him. Cary brightened at once. They were talking animatedly to each other in comic voices when Rosemary left the kitchen.

She went through the hall and out onto the drive in front of the house. She wished it were warm enough to sit out, but a minute or two in the wind convinced her that it wouldn't be possible. She looked around and thought the place must be pretty in the summer, when the rosebushes would be in bloom and there would be foliage on the trees. Now it looked bare and forlorn, leaf buds barely swelling on the thin branches, the only flower an occasional daffodil in the long grass. The pine trees looked heavy with shadows, and Rosemary found she positively disliked the dark rhododendrons farther down the drive. It was a cold, gray landscape in which the elegant white house seemed out of context. It should have had summer and flowers and waving green trees and people with beautiful old clothes, the ladies in skirts which trailed across the grass and the men in kneebreeches and embroidered waistcoats. Like a costume film.

"You're crazy to stay out here without a coat," Bran said, joining her.

"I was going to get a cardigan. Only I don't want to go upstairs while that woman's there."

"Weird old piece, isn't she? When she was going on about Nancy someone or other, I'd have sworn she could be a witch."

"I hated her," Rosemary said.

"She's just nasty. If I'd been Philip, I'd have told her to bugger off and leave us to get on with it."

"I suppose it's difficult, when she's known his uncle and all that."

" 'O my prophetic soul! My uncle!' " Bran said. He saw Rosemary's look and laughed. "You're surprised every time you discover that I've read anything except textbooks on anatomy, aren't you? Do you think you're the only one who's heard of Shakespeare around here?"

"You know him better than I do."

"He's my discovery. Didn't you know? No one in the whole wide world had ever heard of Will S. until little Roy Branwell found a dusty volume hidden in an attic and recognized genius. Only it wasn't a dusty volume, it was a school prize my dad won. Never read a word of it, doesn't like poetry. So when I took it off to read under the bedclothes, he didn't even notice."

"But Bran! You weren't . . . I mean, lots of other people had read Shakespeare before . . ."

He laughed out at that. "Love, all I'm saying is that if a book's put into your hand and you're told, 'This is great lit, you've got to enjoy it,' you don't take so much notice of it as if you find it out all by yourself. Ugh!" He shivered. "I'm going in. It's too much like winter out here. You'll come too if you've any sense."

"I wanted to go for a walk."

"In this weather? You are crazy."

She couldn't explain her need to get away from the house, and the people in it. She said, "I'm going to the village."

"Come back soon."

She fetched her coat from the hooks by the back door. Once out of the drive, she turned left, the way they'd driven in that first day, and along the lane that curved around the side of the hillside on which, out of sight now, the house had been built. The lane went downhill and twisted more than Rosemary had remembered. Above the black bare twigs of the hedges all she could see was the hill, rising gray above her on one side, and the sky, a paler, more uniform gray on the other. And Bran had been right—it was cold. She walked faster and gradually began to feel a little warmth beneath her coat. Her hands remained icy, however, and though she put them in her pockets, they were still red and stiff by the time she reached the crossroads. She turned right and ten minutes later she was walking down the village street.

She had come here because she needed a goal for her solitary walk. Now she was here she might as well buy something. There were small Cox apples in the window of the greengrocer's and she went in. They could always do with more apples—good to munch when you got stuck with reading or an essay. The shop was empty of customers, but the woman with the blue eyes and the pincushion cheeks was behind the counter, unpacking oranges from a box. She smiled at Rosemary.

"Didn't you get your milk?" she asked.

"Yes, we did, thanks."

"What'll it be today, then?"

"Two pounds of apples. The little ones. The Coxes."

The woman took the scoop of the weighing machine and went over to the window to fill it with apples. She said, "They don't look up to much, but they're good. Better than those big, showy ones."

"My dad says there isn't a better apple in the world," Rosemary said.

"I've never eaten any as good, that's certain. These French and Italian jobs, they cost more, but they aren't worth biting into, that's what I think."

She came back to the counter and put the scoop on the machine.

"It's a bit over the two pound. Will you take it like that, or shall I take one or two off?"

"Like it is, please."

"Anything else?"

"How much is the celery?" Bran loved celery, but it had been an impossible price lately.

"Should be twenty pence the head, but it's not up to much. Say ten?"

"That'd be great! Thanks!"

The woman wrapped the head of celery in a sheet of newspaper.

"You managing to keep warm up at the house?" she asked.

"Some of the time. Mostly we sit in the kitchen. The stove there's really good."

"Mr. Peter had that kitchen done over when he got married. Mrs. Edmund, that was his wife, she said she'd never have been able to live in the house if it hadn't been for having the kitchen warm to come into in the mornings."

"Didn't they have fires in the fireplaces? Proper fires. When they were living there all the time?" Rosemary asked.

"They did. But the rooms always seemed cold however much wood they burned," Nancy Rammage said.

"Do you know the house well?" Rosemary asked.

"I've lived here in the village all my life, so I should say yes, shouldn't I? But I don't. Not really. Not like my mother. She worked there on and off for years. I told you. When old Mr. Edward was alive."

"Did your mother live up there?"

"Live there? Of course she didn't."

"I didn't know. I'm sorry." Rosemary didn't know what she was apologizing for.

"There's no need to be sorry. You couldn't know."

"Know what?"

Nancy Rammage hesitated. Then she said, "It's never been the way of anyone from down here to live up at the house. Daily help, it's always been." She hesitated again as if she could have said more, then decided not to.

"Like Mrs. Eye?" This question was not entirely without guile. Rosemary wanted to find out if Nancy Rammage liked Mrs. Eye any better than Mrs. Eye liked her.

"She's up there now. Isn't she?" Nancy Rammage said.

"She came while we were having lunch. Used she to work in the house when your mother did?"

"She did not. Never set foot inside it till after Mr. Peter's wife died. Then when my mother found it too much to go up the hill, she said she'd go in once or twice a week. Said she needed the money, being a widow. Mr. Peter didn't like to refuse her. That's how she got her foot in the door."

Rosemary, answering the tone of this, said, "I didn't like her."

"You're not the only one," Nancy Rammage said.

"Partly why I came out this afternoon was because she's in the house."

"You didn't ask her to come? None of you?"

"No!"

"Tell her to go off, then."

"It's Philip's house. We can't, unless he does."

"And he's like his uncle, I expect. Can't say right out what he wants and what he doesn't?"

"That's right," Rosemary said, thinking of Philip and Cary.

"Mr. Edward was like that too. According to my mother. Once let the painter do over the dining room all blue because he didn't like to tell them once they'd started. And it was a color he couldn't stand. Funny, that!"

"I'm muddled about that Mr. Edmund. You said Edward . . ."

"He was Mr. Edward Edmund. Muddling, isn't it?"

"Philip said he was Mr. Peter's uncle, not his father. Is that right?"

"That's right."

"But why didn't he leave the house to his own children? Mr. Edward, I mean."

"He didn't have any of his own."

"What about his father? Was he . . . did he have the house before that?"

"For a time, he did. He got it from his brother, though."

"It's funny, isn't it? Such a lot of uncles and nephews. I thought houses always went from fathers to sons."

"Not Winter's End. That's how your Philip comes to have the place," Nancy Rammage said. Rosemary wanted to say, "He's not my Philip." But she felt she'd gossiped enough. She said, "I ought to be getting back."

"You'll be down again, I daresay."

"Sure. And thanks for the celery."

"Enjoy it. Bye-bye."

Rosemary called, " 'Bye," as she left the shop and began the trudge back. The gray afternoon had become grayer; she felt she could almost see the night creeping in. When she came to the crossroads she felt an irrational dislike of the blank finger of the signpost pointing along the dark lane which led towards the house and seemed to be sinking into the hills as their sides rose above the high hedges. The telephone wire, supported on bleak, black posts along the way, sang in the wind, a tuneless, wavering, but persistent song. That too was disturbing. More disturbing still was the idea that at any moment she might meet Mrs. Eye, coming away from the house. She didn't want to meet her at all, anywhere, least of all here, between the high hedges and the looming hills, alone. She hurried as much as she could, and she met no one.

She found only Bran and Veryan in the kitchen. Over mugs of tea, she asked, "Has that woman gone?"

Veryan looked at her quickly, but it was Bran who answered. "Left half an hour ago."

"Did she tidy up everything?"

"Took me half an hour to get my room to rights again," Bran said.

"Did she do yours?" Rosemary asked Veryan.

"No."

"You mean she didn't tidy it?"

"She didn't come in."

"How did you manage to stop her?" Rosemary asked, astonished.

"I just sat there."

"Did you say you didn't want her to come in?"

"No."

"And she just went away again?"

"Yes."

"That's what you should have done. Not told her, just gone and kept guard," Bran said to Rosemary.

"It wouldn't have worked if I'd done it," Rosemary said.

"Oh? You think there's something special about Veryan?"

She didn't say so, but Rosemary did.

7

"What's the matter with you?" Bran asked, exasperated.

"I'm sorry."

"Don't be sorry. Just tell me what's the matter?"

"I don't know. I can't seem . . ."

He was angrier than Rosemary had ever seen him. "I don't know what you want. I thought you said to come here tonight. . . ."

"I didn't know it was going to be like this."

"If you didn't want me, you didn't have to say you did."

"It's just . . . I'm sorry, Bran."

She couldn't explain because she didn't understand it herself. The night before it had been Bran who hadn't quite made it. Tonight she couldn't relax. When he came near her, she was shivering, rigid. She'd wanted to be welcoming, grateful for his patience and care last night, loving. And now all she could do was to close up, to keep him out.

"It isn't that I don't want . . ."

"You don't know what you want. It certainly isn't me."

"I do! I do!" It was true. She wanted him physically, and even more she wanted not to hurt him, to be able to reassure him after last night's failure.

"You've a funny way of showing it."

Tears oozed out from under her lids. She was miserable for Bran and for herself.

"For Chrissake, don't *cry*. I can't stand girls who cry."

"I'm miserable."

"So what? What good's that going to do either of us?"

She said again, "I'm sorry."

"And don't keep saying you're sorry."

There was nothing she could say. They lay side by side, their bodies forced to touch by the narrowness of the bed. Bran was angry. He felt cheated. He'd thought yesterday that Rosemary had accepted his failure, that it wouldn't change what she felt about him, any more than it changed what he felt about her. Now he began to class her with the girls who saw sex as a conquest, a lover as another scalp to add to their collection. Who saw a failure as a reflection on themselves.

His mind told him that this wasn't true of Rosemary, but his outraged senses wanted to believe that it was.

A door somewhere along the corridors shut softly. He

felt Rosemary stiffen and remain tense.

"What are you so jumpy for? No one's going to come in here."

She didn't answer.

"Well? Are they? You aren't expecting anyone after me, are you?" He wanted to hurt.

"I thought . . . I did tell Veryan that if she had another nightmare she could come and find me."

"That bloody kid! It was her broke us up last night."

"She couldn't help having a nightmare."

"She didn't have to bawl out like that." Bran knew he was being unreasonable and unfair, but that was how he felt like being. He felt mean towards everyone, Rosemary too. She was still tense and listening, he could tell. There were no more sounds beyond the door, but her mind was out there. Not with him.

He rolled away from her and out onto his feet beside the bed. In the blackness her voice sounded small and lost. "You going?"

"Any reason why I should stay?"

Rosemary would have liked to say, "For comfort." But she couldn't.

"We don't have much luck, do we?" Bran said, feeling for his coat and slippers. He heard Rosemary sniff, and his anger rose in him like sexual excitement. He'd have liked to hit out at someone or something. Instead he had to be quiet and careful. He felt his way to the door and left, without another word. Back in his own room, trying to warm up the bed that felt so cold after Rosemary's, Bran was angry with himself as well as with her. This time it was Rosemary who'd mucked it all up, but under his disappointment he knew that she hadn't been able to help herself. It had been almost as bad for her as for him. Question now was, were they going to try again?

At the moment it didn't feel like it. She'd be put off by this second failure, and it hadn't done him any good either. "I'll be the one to have nightmares tonight," he thought. And he wouldn't be able to go to Rosemary's room for reassurance. Deadlock.

His feet were lumps of ice. He got out of bed, put on a pair of socks, and got back in again. After a time he slept. No dreams.

He deliberately delayed going down the next morning, not wanting to find himself alone with Rosemary. He waited till he'd heard several pairs of feet clatter down the stairs before he emerged from his bedroom. In the kitchen he found Jamie and Veryan sitting at the table with Rosemary. Veryan, silent as usual, was chipping the shell off a boiled egg. Jamie had a plate piled with bacon, sausages, and fried egg. Rosemary, who after a quick look at his face as he came in avoided his eye, was drinking coffee.

"Hullo, there!" Jamie greeted him.

Bran said, "Hi!" and weighed the coffeepot in his hand.

"There's plenty of bacon," Jamie said helpfully.

"Don't want any," Bran said.

"Have a couple of eggs."

"No. Thanks."

"Breakfast. Best meal of the day," Jamie said.

Bran didn't answer this as he sat at the table with his mug of coffee.

"Always make my own breakfast when I'm up," Jamie said.

Perversity made Bran raise his eyebrows and repeat the word: "Up?"

"During term. In college."

"I thought you had everything done for you in that sort of place."

"Nowadays? Good heavens, no! There aren't enough bedders to go around. . . ."

"Bedders?" This was an expression he genuinely didn't know.

"You know. They come in to clean around. Used to make the beds in the good old days. Bring you your meals and everything. What do you call them, then?"

"Not being in an ancient foundation for the sons of gentlemen, we don't have such things," Bran said.

He wasn't surprised that after this Jamie didn't try to pursue the conversation, but ate his eggs and bacon assiduously. When he had finished and had taken his plate over to the sink, he said, looking around, "Anyone seen Cary this morning? Or Philip? They're generally down before this."

"I haven't seen either of them," Rosemary said, when no one else answered.

"Must have been making a night of it," Jamie said, his hand raised between his lips and Veryan to indicate that this was not meant for her to hear. Rosemary saw her lift those great eyes from the table and fix them on her brother with no change of expression, but complete intelligence. She herself looked across at Bran, in an instinctive need for his understanding which she immediately regretted. Of course he wouldn't respond. Not after last night. It was lucky that he hadn't been looking her way. She would have found it difficult to bear the rejection of her appeal.

He was saying, "Philip looked as if he could do with a good long night yesterday." Veryan turned her eyes on him, as if considering this statement, but she didn't speak.

Jamie came back to the table and they sat in silence until the door opened and Cary came in. She was as perfectly groomed as usual, but Rosemary thought that she looked different. Her color was never high, but this morning she was almost pale and there were faint smudges under her beautifully shaped eyes.

"And how's the lovely Cary this morning?" Jamie asked.

"I'm all right."

"We were beginning to wonder where you and Philip had got to."

Cary didn't answer. She poured herself coffee and sat at the table, warming her hands on the mug. She said, "It's freezing upstairs. I can't think how anyone managed to live here right through the winter." Bran, looking at her fingers, red with the cold, thought, "She's got chilled."

"Where's Philip?" Rosemary asked.

"I don't know."

"He isn't ill?"

"Not that I know of."

"Didn't he get up this morning?"

"That's him now," Cary said with obvious relief.

At first sight Philip looked no different from the day before. It wasn't until he was sitting at the table that Bran felt the first prickings of dismay.

"Don't you want any breakfast?" Rosemary asked him, after he had been sitting for a minute or two without making any effort to find either food or drink.

"Breakfast?"

"Breakfast! You're still half asleep," Cary said.

"Coffee'd warm you up," Rosemary said.

"I'm not cold."

"I can't think how you manage not to be. It's icy everywhere except in here."

"Have some coffee, anyway," Bran said. He got up and poured out a mug and put it in front of Philip. "That'll make you feel better."

"I feel all right," Philip said.

"Fine."

"What did you mean that it'd make me feel better?"

"Wake you up. Even if you don't need warming." Bran thought though that Philip certainly did need warming. He, like Cary, looked pinched with cold.

"Why should you think I need waking up?"

"Coffee won't hurt you, even if you don't," Bran said, tired of the conversation.

"What do you mean, it won't hurt me?"

"For Chrissake! I just said that. It didn't mean anything."

"It must have meant something."

"It didn't. It's just a way of speaking."

"You think there's something wrong with me, or you wouldn't talk about making me better. There isn't anything wrong with me. I'm perfectly all right."

Bran said, "Good," and to his relief Philip dropped the stupid argument. Later in the morning, however, when he was reading with admiration the complicated methods by which the human body chemistry keeps itself in balance, he had the feeling that tells one that one is being observed. He lifted his head and saw Philip's eyes fixed on him. Nothing very special about that, he often found he'd been staring at someone without thinking, without seeing the person properly more often than not. But this gaze of Philip's was different. It was steady. It was conscious. And Philip didn't immediately look away. He kept his eyes on Bran with a persistent intensity that was unnerving. This was not the absent stare of the contented daydreamer. Whatever Philip's thoughts were, they were not happy. In spite of the warmth of the room where he'd been sitting for the last two hours, Philip still looked cold. And worse than cold. He looked, Bran thought, tormented. Like a prisoner who has been long locked away from warmth and light and affection. "Lazarus must have looked like that when he came back from the dead. I wonder what he told his sisters when they asked him what he'd seen." The next minute Philip had looked down again at the book he was holding, and Bran had begun to feel that he'd been a fanciful idiot. Philip had been a bit het up this morning, probably because of Cary's putting the pressure on. That was all.

He looked at the others. Jamie, he noticed, spent more time ruffling through the leaves of his book, drumming his fingers on the table, and glancing out the window than he did on his actual reading. Cary was making notes on the margin of her textbook. She'd completely recovered her looks—she was pink and composed again. Rosemary kept her head bent over the essay paper in front of her so assiduously that Bran suspected her of a determination not to look at him. He realized that he was right when she did raise her head and their eyes met. She was crimson immediately and looked away. Bran felt a mixture of regret and exasperation. He knew it hadn't really been her fault last night. He'd been unfair, treating her as if she was a tease. But he still felt the damage to his self-esteem, and he wasn't ready to make any overtures towards peace.

Before going back to physiology, Bran's glance wandered on to Veryan, sitting on the wicker chair behind Cary. She had a book open on her knees, but she was not reading. Instead her eyes were fixed on Philip with the same watchful intensity that Rosemary had noticed two days earlier. For as long as he cared to look, the kid never took her eyes off Philip. He didn't look once at her. There was no question of secret eye messages there. It seemed that all Veryan wanted was to keep looking. What a funny kid. Eventually Bran gave it up, and engrossed himself again in his work. Before his attention had been completely taken up, however, he thought how convenient it would be if the fluctuations of the human emotions could be regularized as quickly and as neatly as the changes in the salt or water contents of the physical body. If they had been, he wouldn't be feeling sour and disagreeable this morning, Rosey wouldn't be miserable. And Philip? He hoped that whatever had got into Philip this morning would get out again quickly. Lazarus could hardly have been a cheerful companion after his return from the grave.

8

Lunch was a more cheerful meal than might have been expected. Bran made large quantities of steaming-hot soup, and even Philip relaxed and joined in the general conversation. They made a list of what someone should buy in the village in the afternoon. The next day would be Sunday, when there'd be no shops open.

"Why don't we walk somewhere tomorrow? Have lunch at a pub?" Bran suggested.

"In this weather?" Cary shivered.

"Might get warmer by then."

"I'm not walking if it's like this. We could drive somewhere, though."

"Six of us are going to be a fair crowd in that car," Bran said.

"Anyway, where'd we walk to? What's the country like around here? Is there anything to see?" Jamie asked.

"Phil? Is there anything to see?"

"I don't remember."

"Any good pubs?"

"How would I know? I told you, I haven't been here since I was a kid."

"We could ask in the village this afternoon," Bran said.

"Who's going?" Cary asked.

"You'll have to because of the car," Jamie said to Bran.

"Right. I'd better have someone else as well in case I can't stay parked anywhere." Rosemary noticed that he didn't ask her if she'd like to come too. She felt relieved, but at the same time missed the being asked. She didn't look at him, pretended to be engrossed in cutting a slice of bread.

"I'll come. Anyway I need some shampoo," Cary said.

"Room for me too?" Jamie asked.

"Please yourself."

"What about you?" Philip said to Rosemary.

"She was there yesterday," Cary said quickly.

"I don't want to go," Rosemary said.

"What was all that yesterday about the Nancy woman ordering in the food for us? Why did the old Eye person get into such a tizzy about it?" Cary asked Philip.

"I don't know."

"I got the impression she thought her traditional rights here were being interfered with," Jamie said.

101

"Mrs. Rammage in the village told me she never started working here till after Philip's uncle's wife had died," Rosemary said.

"What else did she say?" Jamie asked.

"She doesn't like her. From what she said I think Mrs. Eye sort of pushed in, and Mrs. Rammage didn't like it, because of it having been her mother who'd worked up here for Philip's uncle."

"Why was it your uncle who left you the house? Why didn't he leave it to his own children?" Jamie asked, as Cary had asked before. But Philip's reaction this time was different. He said, "Why shouldn't he leave it to me? Do you mean you think I haven't a right to it?"

"Of course not. I only meant places like this are generally entailed, aren't they? So they have to go to the next person in line. . . ."

"This isn't entailed, or whatever you call it. My uncle could have left it to anyone. He happened to leave it to me."

"That means you could leave it to anyone you liked, then," Cary said.

"He could leave it to a cat's home," Bran said, hoping to ease the tension caused by Philip's unaccountable touchiness.

"Or to me. I'm much more deserving than cats," Jamie said, recovering his poise.

"Philip's uncle didn't have any children. So Philip was next in line anyway. Philip'll leave the house to his son. Won't you?" Cary said.

"I might. I don't have to," Philip said.

102

"It'd be pretty mean if you didn't. After all, as they say, you can't take it with you," Jamie said.

"What d'you mean?"

"Well, like they say. You can't take it with you."

"Take it where to?"

"Heaven. Or the other place," Jamie said.

"You're thinking about my being dead."

"Shut up! Of course he's not. He's not serious," Bran said, desperate to put an end to this lunatic exchange. He was the more annoyed when Cary asked him, "Wouldn't you think it was mean if your father cut you out of his will?" and he answered shortly. "If that's how he felt, I don't suppose the will would come as all that of a surprise." When his dad died, there wouldn't be much to write into a will. Except for the farm, and that would go to Johnny, who'd lived and worked there since he left school. What Bran would inherit was what he already had, built into his mind, into his muscles: perfect health and the determination to succeed.

"Wouldn't you mind if your father didn't leave you anything?" Cary asked Jamie. "Why the hell can't she let the subject drop? She has the sensitivity of a rhinoceros," Bran thought, and then wondered if Cary had ever before been compared, even in someone's mind, with a rhinoceros. He guessed not.

Jamie didn't answer at once. Bran saw Veryan look at Jamie as if she were waiting to hear his reply, as if she didn't know what he might say. He wondered if Jamie didn't get on with his father, if Cary had unknowingly touched on a sore point. Jamie's answer, when it came, was noncommittal. He said, "Yes, I expect I'd be fairly annoyed about it."

"I don't even know what your father does. What's his . . . profession? His business?" Cary asked.

There was another, longer pause. When Jamie said, "He's a business consultant. Don't ask me what that means exactly, because I've never understood," his tone was dismissive. Clear that he wasn't going to enlarge on the subject, and, indeed, he changed it immediately. "So, who's for the village this afternoon? Cary and me and Bran, of course. You coming?" he asked Philip.

"I don't know." Philip looked at Cary, but her eyes were fixed on Jamie.

"What about you?" Bran said to Veryan who, as usual, hadn't spoken throughout the meal.

"No, thank you."

He smiled at her, and she slowly smiled back. She really was a funny kid, Bran thought. He'd never met one her age who managed to keep so quiet without giving the impression of sulkiness. He didn't forget that he had a grudge against her, but he had to agree with Rosey that she hadn't done it on purpose. It had been his bad luck that she'd interrupted their lovemaking the night before last and buggered it up, however innocently, last time around.

Rosemary saw the four of them go off in the car an hour later, Philip sitting silent beside Bran, Cary and Jamie animated and teasing in the back. From the window of her bedroom she watched the car disappear down the drive, then wondered what to do with herself. It

104

wasn't that she hadn't got plenty of work, but she didn't feel like doing it. She put on her thick jacket and went out of the house. No point in going towards the village. At the end of the drive she turned right instead of left and followed the winding lane around the side of the hill away from the village.

She was surprised when the ground flattened out enough to afford the space for a churchyard of mossed gray stones surrounding a small gray church with a squat gray stone tower. The lych gate was open and Rosemary walked in.

She read the inscriptions on several of the older, taller and plainer stones. Mary Eliza Minton born 1777, died 15 December 1848, loved, cherished, a pious and affectionate mother and wife. John Stevenson, born 1790, died 1820. Not all that old, then. He'd left a loving wife. A whole family of Robertsons, beginning with Henry and Jane in the mid-1700s and going down to what must have been their great-grandchildren in 1880. A lot of the children had died very young, babies really. Awful to have so many babies and see them die. One of the Robertson couples, Sarah and Joseph, had lost six children in eight years. The oldest had been two. Rosemary was glad that sort of thing didn't happen nowadays. Not in England. It did still in places like Bangladesh and Ethiopia. How did you manage, how did you go on, knowing you'd have a baby every year and knowing it would die? She didn't know the answer.

She went into the church. It wasn't startlingly beautiful; just a fairly ordinary, plan little country church, with

105

bad stained glass over the altar and plain glass in the other windows. A nice wooden roof, solid stone pillars, a flagged floor into which more memorial tablets were set. One wall boasted several white marble slabs and she went across to read them. Sure enough, one of them belonged to Philip's family: a long one, headed by a wreath. She read the list of names below.

IN MEMORIAM

PERCIVAL EDWARD EDMUND
of this parish
born 18 July 1798, died 13 September 1863
and of his wife ANNE CHARLOTTE
born 5 February 1800, died 15 August 1851
this memorial was erected by their surviving children
EDWARD, ANNE, FRANCIS, and CHARLES
It Is Good for a Man That He Bear the Yoke in His Youth

ALSO of their infant daughters
MARY, born 1 January 1839, died 17 July 1840,
and KATHERINE, born 10 October 1840, died 18 February 1841

EDWARD PERCIVAL EDMUND
eldest son of the above
born 6 July 1828, died 3 December 1888
He Was Cut off out of the Land of the Living
and of his wife, JANE
born 16 December 1841, died 25 September 1899

106

THOMAS EDWARD EDMUND
nephew to the above
born 29 June 1860, died 13 May 1907

NICHOLAS FAVERSHAM EDMUND
son of FRANCIS EDMUND
born 3 September 1861, died 20 September 1925
Yet a Little Sleep, a Little Slumber
and of his wife MIRIAM
born 20 May 1870, died 3 January 1943

EDWARD PERCIVAL EDMUND
eldest son of the above
born 24 June 1890, died 29 November 1949
and of his wife, EVELEEN
born 22 August 1898, died 21 April 1953

PATRICIA HELEN EDMUND
dearly beloved wife of PETER EDMUND
born 12 March 1932, died 14 February 1967
also the infant daughter of the above
born and died 12 February 1967

The most recent addition was,

PETER PERCIVAL EDMUND
nephew of the above EDWARD PERCIVAL EDMUND
born 2 July 1916, died 29 November 1976
Sunt Geminae Somni Partae

Rosemary contemplated this for some time. The first Edmund, the one who, according to the rather harsh text chosen—presumably—by his children, had borne the yoke in his youth, must have been the great-great-grandfather of Philip's who had made his money in the north and built Winter's End. She tried to work out how many greats should go before the grandfather, but was muddled by the fact that although sometimes sons seemed to have succeeded their fathers, others were nephews like Philip. Working backwards from the present, she realized that Peter could only have been Philip's father's elder brother; the Edward Percival who'd preceded him must have been the older brother of Peter's father, who'd have been Philip's grandfather. He was one of the inheriting sons; father and mother were the Nicholas and Miriam who had lived here at the turn of the century. So Nicholas was Philip's great-grandfather. Then who was the Francis Edmund who'd been Nicholas' father? Was he the "surviving" Francis, son of Percival Edward? He wasn't, apparently, buried here. And how did Thomas Edward fit in? He also wasn't a son, he was a nephew. She thought Nancy Rammage had said something about a brother inheriting. And remembering the conversation over lunch, she wondered if all the owners of the place had quarreled with their sons and disinherited them in favor of nephews. It was too confusing. She'd ask Philip to explain sometime when he was in a better mood. She turned away from the marble monument towards the open door.

Through the doorway she saw a movement. Something dark was stirring among the still stones outside. She had

108

a moment's panicky fear. But a ghost wouldn't be dark—would it? Or walk about in daylight, even fading daylight? More likely someone from the village. "As long as it isn't Mrs. Eye," she thought. Trying to feel brave, she went out.

Standing in the little porch she could see nothing that moved. The churchyard was as still as the dead it housed. She looked to right and to left, but there was no flicker of life, no indication that there was any other living thing besides herself in the whole gray landscape before her.

She was turning towards the gate when she saw it. The same dark object, motionless now, spread on one of the horizontal slabs of stone. She took a step towards it and recognized Veryan's outsize dark-blue jersey. When she reached the gravestone, she saw that Veryan was lying on it, on her back. Her eyes were shut, but Rosemary knew she wasn't asleep.

She said, "Veryan!" and the tawny eyes opened and looked at her. But Veryan didn't move.

Rosemary wasn't sure how to deal with the situation. "Isn't it cold, lying on the stone like that?"

Veryan said, "Yes," but didn't get up. Rosemary stood by her, uneasy. She had no idea what to say or do next.

"You might catch a cold" was the poor best she could offer.

Veryan sighed and slowly got off the stone and stood up. The slab she'd been lying on was inscribed with the names of Jonathan and Mary Simmonds, who had died of a fever within days of each other in 1772. "In their death they were not divided."

"Were you tired?" Rosemary asked. She couldn't

think of any possible reason for wanting to lie on a stone in a churchyard in this weather.

"No."

Veryan walked carefully between the graves. Now and then she stopped and read an inscription. Rosemary watched her, uneasily. At length Veryan came back to where she was waiting and asked her, "What do you think it's like to be dead?"

"Was that what you were trying to find out?"

"Yes."

Rosemary said cautiously, "I don't believe we go to heaven and all that."

"I meant, like these people. Not playing harps and meeting your . . . friends, but really dead. Like here. Under the ground."

"I don't know. I suppose I think you wouldn't know anything about it."

Veryan said, "Yes." She looked around and said, "It's quiet," in a voice which matched the words. There was no wind to ruffle the branches of the black yew which stood sentinel at the lych gate. The only color in the scene came from a forsythia, flowering late with an extravagant profusion of yellow blossoms that almost deceived the eye into believing that it was irradiated by the sun. Beyond the low gray stone wall the hills smoldered, shadowed and bare.

"Is Philip's uncle buried here?"

"There's a memorial to a lot of the family in the church. I was looking at it just now. Do you want to see it?"

110

They walked side by side back into the church. Veryan stood reading the names of the former Edmunds in her usual silence. At last she said, "Some of them weren't very old when they died."

"People live longer now," Rosemary said.

Still with her eyes on the marble slab, Veryan said, "Did Jamie say anything about Mum and Dad?"

Surprised, Rosemary said, "What about them?"

"Didn't he say anything?"

"I think he told Philip that they weren't going to be at home, so you couldn't stay with them."

Veryan said, "They're dead."

"*What?*"

"They died. On January the twenty-seventh."

Rosemary said, "No!" rejecting the fact before she'd taken it in.

Veryan said, "Yes," still not looking at Rosemary.

"How . . . ?"

"It was on the M 6. Dad often had to go up north. It was one of those foggy days. It wasn't his fault. A lorry ran into the car from behind. They said it would have been quick, the way they died. Instantaneous."

"But . . . why didn't Jamie tell us? He's never said anything. He talks about them as if they were . . . alive."

"I know. He won't say that they're dead. I think he's sort of pretending they're still alive . . . somewhere."

"Where were you when . . . when it happened?"

"At school."

Rosemary stared at her. She tried to imagine what it

would be like to come home at the end of the school day and to find the house empty. Or to find strangers there, waiting to tell the news. Or perhaps to be called at mid-morning into the headmistress's study, to hear her say, "I'm sorry to have to tell you, Rosemary, that there's been an accident. Your mother and father were both killed instantaneously." She'd had nightmares, occasionally, about something like this. But to this girl in front of her it had really happened. She said, "What did you do?" and heard her voice despairing.

Veryan looked at her now. "What could I do?"

"I don't know. I don't know what anyone does." Rosemary found that she no longer thought of Veryan as Jamie's kid sister. She was speaking to her as she would have to a contemporary.

"At first I didn't believe it. When I woke up in the mornings I didn't always remember. . . . That was horrible. And people kept on saying things. About being brave. About not brooding. You know how they do."

Rosemary nodded.

"I think I was trying to be like that at first. Being brave and not crying. And then . . ."

"What happened?" Rosemary asked.

"One day I knew I was . . . pretending. To myself."

"Do you mean, like Jamie? That your mother and father weren't . . . were still alive?"

"More that I didn't mind. But I did. Mind."

Rosemary said, "Of course you minded." It sounded hopelessly inadequate, but she didn't want to push other words into what Veryan was saying. She didn't want to be one of the voices telling her to be brave, to pretend.

"So I let myself know that I minded."

"I'm really sorry," Rosemary said. Veryan turned those deep-water eyes on her again.

"Some people who don't tell you to be brave think you have to talk about it all the time."

"Don't you want to talk about it at all?"

She considered this. "I do sometimes. Like now. I wanted you to know. I don't like it the way Jamie wants. Talking about . . . them as if they were still alive. But that doesn't mean you can't talk about anything else."

"You don't talk much about anything," Rosemary said.

"I don't know any of you very well."

"Can't you talk to Jamie?"

"Not about Mum and Dad. Not now."

"What happens if you try?"

"He won't listen. He says not to be morbid. But it isn't being morbid. Pretending is like saying that nothing's happened, nothing's changed. It's almost like saying that I didn't have any feelings about them when they were there."

She looked back at the tablet on the wall.

"All of them must have been quite old when their fathers and mothers died."

"Not Philip's aunt Patricia. Right at the end, the bottom but one. She was . . . thirty-five, and the baby died too."

"A lot of them didn't have children," Veryan said.

"Or the children weren't buried here."

"I wouldn't want to have a baby in that house," Veryan said.

"Why not?" Rosemary was surprised.

"It's cold."

"You could light a lot of fires in the big rooms."

"I didn't mean that sort of cold."

"What sort of cold, then?"

She hesitated before she said, "You don't feel as if you were wanted there. The house doesn't want you. Not really."

"Doesn't want you?"

"You know what I mean. It's not a . . . friendly house. It looks as if it was going to be, but when you get inside it isn't."

Rosemary remembered what she'd said to Bran. That she didn't want to make love there—she felt spied on, watched. She'd thought it was because of Cary. Perhaps it wasn't only Cary. Perhaps there was something about the house. It certainly didn't seem to have done them, her and Bran, much good.

The flagged path beyond the door had darkened and was glistening wet. A steady fine drizzle was falling from the heavy sky. Rosemary said, "It's raining. We'd better get back."

Veryan followed her out of the church, past the stones and crosses commemorating the long dead, between the yews and out into the road. They walked for a little without speaking, then Veryan said, "Will you tell Philip? About my mum and dad?"

"Do you want me to?"

"Yes, please."

Rosemary remembered the impression she'd had, the day Jamie and his sister had arrived, that Veryan didn't like Philip. She said, "Right. I will. Do you want me to tell the others?"

"You can tell Bran."

"What about Cary? No, I suppose Philip will tell her."

"No. He won't," Veryan said.

"What do you mean?"

"I don't think he talks to her," Veryan said, and Rosemary realized that she was right. She couldn't imagine Cary listening to Philip, asking him questions and waiting for the answers. She couldn't imagine them sharing secret, stifled laughter as she and Bran had in bed together. She thought suddenly with a great warmth of Bran, how he'd stroked her, how he'd held her in his arms. All right, their lovemaking hadn't been a great success, but he'd given her something that she suspected Cary and Philip had never had. What? Difficult to put a name to. Warmth, being able to give and to take, being sure of each other. She wished he were here with her now. But he was angry with her, he hadn't spoken to her all day. She hoped the quarrel wasn't going to last too long.

Thinking of the night that had begun so well for them, she said to Veryan, "You haven't had any more nightmares?"

"No."

"No dreams at all?"

Veryan said, "Yes, dreams. I'm a very strong dreamer." She didn't enlarge on this remark, and though Rosemary wasn't sure what it meant, she didn't ask for an explanation.

9

The problem, Rosemary thought, of telling Philip what Veryan had told her was that she never saw him alone. Cary was always about. Wherever Philip was, Cary would be seconds later. On one occasion Rosemary met Philip coming out of the bathroom in the upstairs corridor, but she didn't feel that she could immediately open a conversation by saying, "Did you know that Jamie's been lying about his parents? They're dead." She got as far as saying, doubtfully, "Philip?" But when he stopped and looked at her, she hesitated, and a moment later Cary had appeared at the door of her room and was saying, "Phil! Come in here again for a minute, will you?" And of course he went.

Telling Bran seemed as if it might be no easier. Rosemary knew that it was no accident that she hadn't seen him except when the others were about. He wouldn't be tapping that quick, dotted rhythm on her door tonight. He hadn't forgiven her for what had happened the night before. At supper he never looked in her direction, talked to the others but never to her. After the meal, he disappeared. It was only when she heard the car come up the drive, just as she was falling miserably to sleep, that she realized he'd been out for hours. She stayed awake after that for some time, still listening, for what she didn't know. When at last she slept it was a deep but unrefreshing sleep from which she awoke feeling numb.

It was clear at breakfast that that Sunday morning was not going to allow them to go on the proposed expedition. They'd woken to the sound of wind lashing the walls and the roof of the house with angry drenchings of rain. It seemed as if it would never stop; the windows on the north and west sides were blind with streams of water, and the trees and bushes in the garden bent and writhed as if they were trying to escape from the tormenting gale. It was no day for going out. The atmosphere indoors wasn't much better than outside, Rosemary thought when the last one had arrived downstairs for breakfast. Surprisingly, this was Bran, usually one of the first to make an appearance.

"You're late! What did you get up to last night?" Cary greeted him.

"Went to the local."

"How's the beer there?" Jamie asked.

"Lousy. And I had too much of it. Got a headache

that'd crack open a brass monkey."

"You need coffee," Cary said.

"You couldn't be righter. Don't bother. I'll get it."

"Don't be silly. Of course I'll get it for you," Cary said. Rosemary thought, "She wouldn't do that for Veryan or me. Only for a boy." But Bran did look bad. Sallow and heavy-eyed and frowning with the pain. He didn't look her way.

"We aren't going out in this?" Jamie asked through a mouthful of sausage.

"I'm not," Cary said.

"And I'm not driving in this weather," Bran said.

"We can make it tomorrow. If the rain stops," Rosemary said.

"And work again all day? My brain's addled," Jamie said.

"Go out for a walk and get it soaked instead," Bran said.

"Thanks very much."

"Let's listen to the weather forecast and see what they say about tomorrow," Rosemary suggested.

"What's the good? They're always wrong," Cary said.

"Anyway the next one isn't till the one o'clock news."

"It's half past ten now."

"Well? What are we going to do?" Cary asked impatiently.

"I'm going back to bed to sleep this off," Bran said. He picked up his mug of coffee and left.

"I suppose we'll have to work, then. Or make as if we were working," Jamie said.

"You could go to church," Veryan said. It was almost the first time she had volunteered a remark in company, and everyone looked at her with surprise.

"Do you want to go?" Cary asked.

"No. I only said you could."

"It might be something to do. Shall we?" Cary asked Philip and Jamie.

"No, thanks. Not for me," Jamie said.

"Phil?"

He shook his head.

"I'm certainly not going by myself," Cary said.

"All right, then. We work this morning and hope for better things this afternoon," Jamie said, stretching and yawning.

Rosemary left them. She went upstairs towards her own room. Outside Bran's door she hesitated, wondering whether to go in and to try to make her peace with him. But common sense suggested that this would be better done when he wasn't suffering the effects of a hangover, and reluctantly she passed his room and went into her own. She felt out of sorts with the world. Partly because of having slept badly, partly because she'd been disturbed by the conversation with Veryan the day before. Mostly because of Bran. She didn't want to work in the same room as the others. She put on her thickest cardigan, wrapped a blanket around her legs, and began to read.

An hour later, she had to admit that she was too uncomfortable to be able to concentrate. She thought longingly of the warm kitchen, stretched her cramped, chilled arms and legs, and decided that she'd have to put up with the others' company for the sake of warmth. She took

Carlyle downstairs with her. In the kitchen she found Philip, surprisingly alone.

He looked up as she came in, but didn't speak or smile.

"Where are the others?"

He looked around the room as if he hadn't noticed that they weren't there, then said, "I don't know."

Rosemary sat at the table. This was the moment when she must speak. She said, "Philip! Veryan wanted me to tell you something."

He said, "What?" without showing any great interest.

"She says that Jamie's . . . she says that their mother and father are dead."

He stared at her as if he hadn't heard.

"She says they were killed in an accident. In January."

"An accident?"

"A car accident on the M 6. She said."

Philip said, "They're dead." It was not quite a question.

"I told you. Of course they're dead."

"But Jamie said . . ."

"Veryan says that Jamie wants to believe they're still alive. No, not quite like that. It's just that he won't talk about them as if they weren't. But that's why he had to bring Veryan here with him. There's no one at home for her to be with."

"Is that all?"

"What do you mean, is that all?"

"You said you wanted to tell me something," Philip said.

"Isn't that enough? What would you feel like if your

mother and father had been killed in an accident two months ago?"

Philip said, "Yes, I see. They're dead."

Rosemary couldn't understand him. She couldn't believe that he'd really taken in what she'd said. She cried out at him, "Don't you mind?"

He looked at her as if her anger were as incomprehensible to him as she found his indifference. It was unfortunate that at this moment Cary walked into the room. Even if she hadn't heard what they'd said, she couldn't miss the fact that Rosemary was angry. She said sharply, "What's the matter?"

"I was just telling Philip something."

"I thought you were going to work in your room?"

"It's too cold. I had to come down. . . ."

"What were you telling Philip? What was she saying?" Cary asked Philip, who looked at Rosemary and said, "You tell her."

"Veryan wanted me to tell Philip . . ."

"Veryan? What on earth has she got to tell Phil?"

"Her and Jamie's parents are dead. They were killed in a car crash in January."

For a moment Cary didn't speak. Then she said, "That's nonsense. Jamie was talking about his father yesterday."

"Veryan says he doesn't want to admit . . ."

"That's ridiculous! Of course if they're dead Jamie must know. He's not crazy!"

"She didn't say he didn't know, she said . . ."

"I'd believe Jamie much more than I would her. I

think she definitely peculiar. The way she just looks at you and doesn't say anything. Anyway she's a teenager. Everyone knows teenagers invent stories to make themselves more important. I don't believe it's true. You don't, do you, Phil?"

"I shall have to think about it," Philip said.

"I can't see what there is to think about. Just ask Jamie. He'll tell you."

"You can't!" Rosemary said.

"Why not?"

"Because if he doesn't want to talk about it . . . you can't just ask him."

"He'd tell me," Cary said, very sure of herself. Rosemary could imagine just how she'd approach Jamie, ready with sympathy if it were needed, or with quick scornful amusement if it turned out to be nothing but the fantasy of an inconvenient younger sister. Not really feeling anything herself except the desire to impress. Cary was saying now, "I'm sure it's all made up. I'll ask him this afternoon." Looking at Rosemary as if to say, "You won't stop me." Then to Philip she said aloud, "Unless you don't want me to, Phil?"

"Why shouldn't I want you to?" Philip asked.

"Oh, you know. You mightn't like my talking to Jamie."

"Talking to him about what?"

"About this silly story, of course."

"Only about this story?"

"I can't promise we won't talk about anything else, can I?"

"What else?"

"I don't know. Anything else. This lousy weather, for instance. I mean, if he starts talking about something, I can't just walk away. I've got to be polite, haven't I?"

Philip said, "I suppose so."

"No, but really, Phil. I won't saying anything to him if you'd rather I didn't."

Rosemary picked up her book again and tried not to listen to the stupid exchange. Cary was trying to provoke Philip into an admission that he was jealous of Jamie, and was certainly succeeding in making him suspect that she had a great deal more to say to him than she wanted to admit. When at last the argument petered out, she found it still difficult to concentrate on Carlyle's long paragraphs, full of exclamation marks and apostrophes. Bran had said it should be read aloud, but she couldn't do that now. And so, from Carlyle's philosophy, she turned to thinking about Bran. She was missing him. In the first days here he'd become her special companion and ally. Without him she felt immensely alone. She'd never supposed that she and Cary would become friends, but she had counted on Philip as someone she'd like to be with. She liked his quiet sense of humor and he'd always, above everything, been kind. Now he seemed to have lost both his kindness and his humor. Jamie was a show-off, and Veryan . . . too young and too strange to be a real friend. She needed Bran. She longed for him. She didn't know how she could make it up with him. As he'd said, "What's the good of saying you're sorry?" And it wasn't as if it had been all her fault. He'd had his failure too.

It was a lost day. The wind never stopped tearing around the hillside, gusting down on the house and the garden, tormenting the trees and shrubs, and bringing with it rain that fell in spiteful cascades of steel arrowheads, biting against the windows and drumming on the roof. Occasionally the sky lightened for minutes, only to show ragged clouds scudding across the horizon, followed by others, darker and heavier with as yet unspilled water. Bran volunteered after lunch to go down to the village to fetch the Sunday papers if there were any to be had, and came back dismally with one which they shared out, sheet by sheet, sitting around the kitchen, bored with work, bored with their enforced seclusion, bored with each other. Jamie and Cary made a halfhearted attempt to do the crossword puzzle together, but in spite of their frequent appeals to the others for help, they made no progress and soon abandoned the effort. Bran read, hardly lifting his eyes from the printed sheets, smoking his pipe—more for show than for pleasure, Rosemary thought, since he produced it so infrequently. Veryan read a book. Philip held the pages of the paper in front of his face, but once when Rosemary passed his chair and looked more closely at him, she saw that he was not reading. Instead, his eyes wandered from one of his companions to another uneasily, as if his thoughts about them were troubling.

On her way down from a visit to the bathroom just before supper Rosemary found Veryan standing by the great semicircular window above the front portico, looking out into the dark wet night.

"What are you doing?"

Veryan hesitated before she answered, "Nothing, really."

"Supper's nearly ready. Bran's making Welsh rarebit and fried eggs."

"That'll be nice."

Rosemary stared at her. Yesterday she'd felt sorry for her. Passionately sorry. She'd wanted to help. She'd been impressed by Veryan's self-containedness. She'd felt something like awe at Veryan's capacity for solitude and for the certainty she appeared to possess. But now, feeling cramped and irritable and sore about Bran, Rosemary felt annoyed. She felt like blaming Veryan for everything that had gone wrong between Bran and herself. At that moment she saw Veryan only as a lumpy, inconvenient school kid, making stupid remarks. Possibly Cary was right, and she was hysterical into the bargain, and none of this story about her parents was true. Rosemary knew she wasn't being fair. She didn't want to be fair

She wanted to hurt. She said, "I told Philip what you said."

"Did he . . . ? Did he say anything?"

"Not really."

"Nothing?"

"I'm not sure if he believed it was true." She knew that this was unkind, but she almost didn't care.

"It's true," Veryan said.

"Only it seems so . . . funny that Jamie doesn't say anything about it. I mean, the way he talks . . ."

"You believed me yesterday," Veryan said.

126

"Ye—es. But . . ."

"It isn't Philip. It's Cary. Isn't it?"

"It's Cary who what?"

"Who says it isn't true. Philip didn't say that. Did he?"

"No—o."

It would have suited Rosemary's resentment better if Veryan had protested, had shouted at her, had behaved more dislikably. Instead the girl said only, "It is true," and turned towards the stairs. Rosemary followed her into the kitchen and saw her take her place, silent as usual, at the table. She felt disappointed, and she didn't like herself for having wanted to hurt. Bran's supper was excellent, but he hardly spoke to her, and after the meal was over he read without looking up from his book until he went to bed. Rosemary felt fed up with everything and everyone, including herself.

In the beautiful white shell of the house, that night, six people lay, separated from each other by sleep. For five of them it was the blank white sleep of utter unconsciousness. Only Veryan struggled with the dark labyrinth of the mind. Only Veryan dreamed.

10

The wind dropped during the night. On Monday morning the house was wrapped in a mist as white as itself. From the windows there was nothing to be seen except filmy outlines of the nearest trees. The ghostly effect was heightened by the silence; even the birds seemed to have been blotted out. Bran looked out of his window and hated what he saw. Like Rosemary the day before, he felt trapped in this cool, elegant prison, where nothing seemed to be going right, not for him nor for anyone else. He didn't know, didn't want to know what was going on between Cary and Philip, but it was quite clear that neither of them was enjoying it. Yesterday he'd thought Philip looked really odd. Not exactly physically ill; more as if he might be heading for a nervous breakdown. What with Jamie overdoing the charm, and the kid sister saying nothing at all, and things in this state between himself and Rosey, Bran couldn't think how he was going to stand another six days being cooped up here. It wasn't even good for his work. There was more than enough time every day for the reading he had to do, but the atmosphere of disquiet and claustrophobia made concentration near impossible.

He dressed quickly. It was surprising how cold these big bedrooms were. There seemed to be more room for drafts than in his own low-ceilinged room in the farm at home. Of course it was a room meant for two, Bran thought. Damn Rosey! She'd spoiled what he'd hoped was going to be something really special. He could have stood the troubles with the other four if he and she had really made it, if he'd had the comfort and pleasure of making love to her every night. Not just for the sex, either. For the companionship, for the fun. He really liked Rosey. That first night, in spite of his failure, he'd felt close to her, he'd loved just holding her satiny body in his arms and feeling her laughter ripple against him.

He'd been unfair. She couldn't help it if the next night she'd been on edge. She wasn't a cheat, a tease. On impulse, he left his room and went and tapped on Rosemary's door. She might have gone down to breakfast already. He didn't know whether he hoped she had or hadn't.

She hadn't. She opened the door almost at once, fully dressed apart from her bare feet and her hair, which was hanging all over her face. She held a brush in her hand.

"Bran!"

She was smaller without the height her shoes gave her, and her unbrushed hair made her look very young. The last of Bran's anger melted away. He smiled at her.

"Forgiven me?"

"I thought it was you who hadn't . . ."

"That's all right, then." He hated long explanations and emotional post mortems. He pushed the hair off her face and kissed the tip of her nose. "Wow! You're freezing. Better come down quickly and warm up."

"I'm nearly ready."

"Shall I wait? We could make a surprise entry as a reconciled couple." But he saw a shadow cross her face and remembered her saying, ". . . us knowing whenever Cary and Philip are together and them knowing about us." He said, "No, I'm not warm enough to hang about. See you downstairs," and left. Feeling astonishingly much better. He paused at the long window that looked out to the front of the house at the top of the stairs to make a face at the blank wall of fog outside, then ran down. He'd be glad to get into the warmth of the kitchen.

It wasn't just the warmth of the kitchen he walked into. It was also the heat of an argument. As he opened the door he heard Jamie's voice raised in protest. "That's absurd, Philip! You can't say things like that!" and Cary quickly intervening, "He didn't mean it like that. Did you, Phil?"

Bran shut the door behind him and looked at the four people sitting at the table. He saw Cary, her color becomingly heightened; he saw Jamie, angry, shaken out of his

130

carefully cultivated social graces. He saw Veryan, silent of course, gazing at Philip with grave, anxious eyes. Philip himself looked more animated than he had the day before, but his eyes were restless. As Bran went past him to pour himself a mug of coffee, Philip said in a voice that sounded faintly querulous, "I just said I can't seem to get any work done here."

"That's not our fault!" Jamie said.

"What are we supposed to be doing? Crowding you out of your own house?" Bran said. Best to treat the argument as a joke. He was surprised that Philip took time to answer as if he were considering this seriously, and then said, "Why would you do that?"

"We wouldn't. I just wanted to know how we prevent you from working?"

Philip said slowly, "I can't be sure . . ."

"Tell me when you find out. It might do me a bit of good too," Bran said, bringing his plate and mug to the table and sitting down.

"You mean you can't work either?"

"I reckon this bloody weather has a lot to do with it. No exercise, and all of us on top of each other all the time," Bran said. Not perhaps the most elegant way of expressing what he meant, he thought. Not even accurate. If he could have been on top of the right person in the right way, the weather wouldn't have interfered with his capacity to work. He glanced around the table to see if anyone else might have picked up the meaning. Not a glimmer. He wished Rosey'd been there. She'd have got it. They could have exchanged a quick look, better than words. He would have ached for her if it hadn't been for that short exchange five minutes ago which had left him with a glow inside that no weather could dim.

The threatened row seemed to have subsided. Cary said, "I don't know why, but I'm terribly sensitive to the weather. I'm never really happy when the sun isn't shining," and Jamie responded with, "That's exactly how I feel!" They were off on a duet of self-exploitation and mutual ego-feeding. Bran stopped listening. Philip seemed to have forgotten his complaint. He was eating, with his eyes on his plate. But the girl, Veryan, was still looking at him. She's like a really young kid, the way she stares, Bran thought. The next moment Rosemary had come into the kitchen, and he forgot everyone else.

He forgot until the end of the morning, when he went out onto the portico steps to clear his mind after two and a half hours of solid work. Quite good work, too. He'd had no problems concentrating this time. The fact that Rosemary was sitting almost within touching distance had proved an incentive instead of a distraction. Outside the house the mist was thinning. He could even see a pale radiance in the sky where the sun was trying to break through. There was a sort of soft stillness quite different from anything they'd yet had since they came here. It certainly wasn't as chillingly cold. At the sound of steps behind him, he turned, hoping it would be Rosey. But it was Philip who had followed him out there.

"Might turn out a decent day," Bran said, sniffing the damp air. It smelled of wet grass and wet bark, not disagreeably.

Philip came to stand beside him.

"Manage to get any work done this morning?" Bran asked.

Philip didn't answer directly. Instead he said, "Why did you say that this morning?"

"Say what?"

"About crowding me out of the house."

"I don't know. Does it matter?"

"I'm not sure. It might be important."

"For Chrissake! It was a joke!" Bran said.

"A joke?"

"You know! You were saying about not being able to work, and I said were we crowding you? Of course it was a joke. How could we crowd you in a house this size?"

"You said crowd me out. As if you wanted to get rid of me."

"For Chrissake . . ." Bran began again when the front door opened and Cary came out.

"O—oh! Cold!" She shivered.

"That's because you've been sitting on top of the stove. It's nothing like as cold as it has been," Bran said, grateful for an excuse to break off the conversation with Philip. He'd always known that Philip was a serious character, but this nitpicking over a chance remark was more than he could stand.

"Why did you come out?" Philip asked her.

"Finished my chapter. And I wanted to see what you were up to."

"Up to? What did you think I'd be up to?"

"I don't know. Catching cold? How do I know what

you mightn't do when I'm not there to look after you?"

"Where are the others? Where's Jamie?" Philip asked abruptly.

"In the kitchen. Rosemary's getting the meal. . . ."

"I'm going to see," Philip said. He went back through the front door, but to Bran's surprise Cary made no effort to follow him. Bran didn't mean to be left alone there with her and he turned towards the door, when Cary stopped him.

"Bran. Wait a minute."

He half expected Cary to make one of her semiserious passes. Instead of which she said uncertainly. "You know what Phil was saying this morning?"

"That load of rubbish?"

"It was, wasn't it?"

"Of course it was. How the hell could we stop him working? If he really wanted to?"

She didn't look entirely reassured. She said, "Sometimes he says things I don't understand."

"Like what?"

"When he started off about not being able to work. I thought he just meant how it is. You know. You have times when you can't seem to think. . . ."

"I know."

"So I said, yes, I know, like you just did, and he sort of turned on me and said it was my fault, I was stopping him."

"Were you? Had you been talking a lot?" Bran's sympathies were with Philip.

"No! I hadn't said a word!"

"Nothing at all for how long? Ten minutes?" Bran asked.

"Ages. Well. About two and a half hours."

"And he said you were interrupting him?"

"Not exactly. He said he couldn't work because of what I was thinking."

"What you were thinking?"

"That's what he said. He said I was interfering with his thoughts by the way I was thinking."

"You must have been saying something."

"I wasn't! I was working."

Bran hardly believed her. Even if she hadn't actually spoken she'd probably somehow managed to keep Philip continuously aware of her presence. A thing Cary was good at doing. He could imagine how tiresome it could be to have an urgent Cary moving, sighing, looking, leaning, when you were trying to concentrate.

"What shall I do?" Cary was asking. She was damnably pretty. When she looked like that, Bran had a nearly overmastering impulse either to spank her or to kiss her. He couldn't tell which was the stronger.

He resisted them both. He said, "Keep your cool and don't let him talk punk." He led the way indoors without looking back. Cary had probably only got what she'd asked for.

11

After lunch Bran drove Rosemary down to the village. Careful this time to give no one else the opportunity of suggesting that they come too.

She sat beside him without speaking, surprised at the lift she'd felt all morning in her heart. She felt extraordinary now. Tremulous with joy. Without turning her head, she slid her eyes sideways and saw Bran's profile; his dark, frowning brows, his knobbly nose, his obstinate mouth and chin. She thought, "What's happened? I've never even been sure whether he's really attractive." She remembered saying to Sheila, "He's interesting, but he's not terribly sexy."

It just showed how wrong you could be. What had she thought then that terribly sexy meant? Looking like the man who advertised someone's low-tar cigarettes on a TV commercial, all hair and capped teeth? Or like the tough guys who swept girls off their feet and into their beds in the movies?

Sexy is as sexy does, Rosemary thought, and laughed out loud.

"Joke?" Bran asked.

"Sort of."

"Tell me."

"Not now."

"When?"

She thought she might tell him that night. In bed. If he came again to her room. Anxiety seeped through her and nudged dangerously at her present serenity. Suppose it was no good again? Suppose one of them mucked it up? Again. She had a horrible moment of wondering how two people ever did get it exactly right together. There were so many things that could go wrong.

In the greengrocer's Nancy Rammage greeted her as an old acquaintance.

"My goodness you get through a lot! Working hard, are you?"

"Some of the time."

"Nasty weather you've been having. Shame. On your holiday, and all."

"We've hardly been out at all."

"Might be getting better. You never know."

She fetched two empty wooden boxes from the back of the shop and began weighing out vegetables.

"Is it the large onions you'll want? Or the little ones?"

"The large ones. Quicker to peel," Bran said. Nancy gave him her slow smile.

"You the cook?" she asked.

"Cordon bleu. Costs you ten quid just to speak to me," he assured her. He left Rosemary with the list and went off to buy stamps and chocolate in the post office next door.

"You getting on all right up there?" Nancy Rammage asked Rosemary when he'd gone.

"We're all right," Rosemary said. True of herself and Bran, but hardly of any one of the others. But this sort of question didn't expect anything but the ordinary conventional response.

"Mr. Philip all right?"

"Why shouldn't he be?"

Nancy Rammage didn't answer this. She seemed to be engrossed in picking out sound carrots and putting them into the scoop from the weighing machine. Coming back to the counter with the metal container, she said, "What do you think of the place now you've been there nearly a week?"

"I haven't seen much of it. It's been so cold. We haven't been out a lot."

"What about the house? What do you make of that?"

"It's very pretty. Beautiful, I suppose. Much too grand for us really."

"It's beautiful all right," Nancy Rammage said. Something about the way she spoke made Rosemary ask, "Is there something wrong with it, then?"

"What should be wrong with it?"

"I thought from the way you said that . . ." She found she was repeating what Veryan had said. "It's cold. It isn't . . . friendly."

"That's right."

"Hasn't it ever been? I mean . . . is it just because no one's been living in it for so long?"

"Mr. Peter only died last year," Nancy Rammage said.

"Was it . . . all right when he was alive?"

"It was different. It seemed as if it might be going to be better . . ." Nancy Rammage said.

"I don't understand. Better than what?"

Nancy Rammage said, "It looked as if there'd be children. A family. She was a lovely lady, Mrs. Peter. When she died it was . . . bad. For us. And of course for Mr. Peter, it was worse. I've never seen anyone like he was then. It was as if he'd died with her. That was how it seemed."

"But . . . how could he let Mrs. Eye go there? She's . . . He didn't like her. Did he?"

"He didn't care about what happened. Or that's how it seemed. And like I told you, he never could say no. Never did. So then the house . . . It was her kind of place after that."

"You mean . . . ? What's her kind of place?" But Nancy Rammage had turned away as if the conversation had finished. She rearranged a couple of tins on the shelf behind her, began, "It's not an easy house to live in . . ." then interrupted herself, and in a different voice said, "There's your boyfriend back already."

The rest of the conversation was about white cabbage,

potatoes, the wicked price of everything, why vegetables cost just as much in the country as in the town. Ordinary, should have been reassuring, but somehow wasn't.

Back in the car as they drove out of the village, Bran said, "What's the matter?"

"Nothing, really."

"Go on. Tell me."

"That Mrs. Rammage. She seemed to be saying something about the house."

"What?"

"She said it wasn't an easy house to live in. What d'you think she meant?"

"Could mean it'd take a lot of work to run."

"She didn't say it like that. More as if . . ."

"As if what?"

"As if there was something funny about it. Not that sort of funny. Peculiar."

"You're being peculiar yourself," Bran said.

"I don't like it. I wish we weren't staying there."

They were approaching the crossroads. Instead of taking the lane which led to the house, Bran forked right.

"This isn't the way back!" Rosemary said.

"You've just said you don't like the house. There's no hurry for us to get back yet," Bran said.

"But we don't know where this road goes to."

"We shall when we've driven along it."

"It might just be a dead end."

"What does it matter? It's not a bad road. Don't fuss so, Rosey. Can't you just go along with it and see what happens?"

The road ran up into the hills above the lower lane that went to Winter's End. It wasn't much of a road after the first mile, and very soon the hedges disappeared and the road itself became more of a track, winding along and up the side of the hill. Below, Rosemary could see nothing of the valley except the mist. It was thinner up here, but enough to hide the tops of the hills. Bran drove slowly and the old car bumped and jolted over the ruts and stones in its way. Suddenly, without warning, they were out, above the cloud, in brilliant sunshine, so dazzling that Rosemary shaded her eyes. Another twenty yards of the track and they had reached the top. Bran stopped the car and got out. Rosemary followed him.

"What about that?" Bran said.

They could see now that the hill they had climbed ran in a great curving sweep before them, encircling the mist-filled valley below. On the farther side the ground fell away sharply down to the flat country through which they'd journeyed the week before. This too was largely obscured by cloud. The effect of standing there, with the sun warm on their backs and the blotted-out landscape beneath, was that they had been miraculously lifted out of their ordinary lives and set down on a mountaintop remote from everyone else. They might have been alone together in the world.

"It's warm! The sun's warm!" Rosemary murmured. She took off her coat and had the feeling which seems new each spring after a winter of huddling into too many clothes in order to keep out the cold—the delicious feeling of warm air on her neck and arms like a blessing. A tiny breeze ruffled Bran's hair and stroked her cheek.

"What are you smiling at?" Bran asked.

"This wind. It's not like the one down there. This one's kind. It won't . . . bite."

"Glad you came?"

"It's lovely."

He put an arm round her shoulders.

"Glad you came here with me?"

"Yes."

He looked at her critically.

"You may be right about the house down there. You look different here."

"I feel different." She did. She felt light, as if a weight had been lifted off her back. Free. Happier than she had for days. She smiled at Bran and stretched her arms above her head. "I feel marvelous. I'm warm!"

"Let's walk a bit. We've got plenty of time."

"Won't they wonder where we are?"

"Let them. What's it matter?" He released her from his arm and turned onto the grass away from the rutted track.

"Aren't you going to lock the car?" Rosemary asked.

"Why should I? There's nobody up here, only us."

They walked side by side on the short turf. The ground was uneven, and here and there, in small hollows, there were bushes and a few small, wind-stunted trees. As they passed one clump, Bran stopped and circled a twig with his thumb and forefinger. "Look! In a week there'll be leaves here."

"It looks dead," Rosemary said.

142

Bran scraped a nail down the side of the small branch. "Course it's not dead. It's green under the brown. Alive. If we came back here next week you'd see. Everything'd look different."

"In a week's time we won't be here," Rosemary said.

"You'll be glad."

"Some ways I will."

"Glad not to have me around?"

"No."

"Sure of that?"

"Mm." Feeling that this didn't sound convincing, she said, "I didn't like your being angry with me."

He began with a denial. "I wasn't . . ." then checked himself. "I was stoopid." He looked at her, moving easily in the sunlight beside him, her coat over her shoulders, her cheeks flushed, the gentle wind molding her pullover against her breasts. He remembered the silky feel of her skin. He put an arm around her and felt the dip of her waist above the hard ridge of the hip bone. He kissed her cheek, deliciously cool and warm at the same time. He pulled her around to face him and kissed her on the mouth. He could feel her momentary hesitation, then her leaning towards him in a sort of consent. With his free hand he undid the front of his own coat and they stood pressed against each other inside the outer skins of their winter coats, warming each other, each hearing one heartbeat drumming in the ears and at the same time aware of the pulsing close in the other body.

Bran said, "Rosey? What about it?"

She said, "Here?" and looked around at the bare hillside with its low prickly bushes and small bent trees. Overhead and out of sight a lark trilled a sharp, ecstatic song.

"It's not too cold," he said.

"Suppose someone comes?" she said, as she had said before.

"Not likely. But anyway . . ." He took her by the hand and led her to one of the little dips in the ground. By bending nearly double, it was possible to dodge the thorns and to clamber inside the ring of bushes to a hollow, just big enough to take two people lying next to each other. Bran took off his coat and put it on the grass and lay on it. Rosemary held back.

"Come on. Rosey, come on."

There was no wind inside the thorn ring. The sun shone down on them through the black branches. Bran's hands were cool and gentle inside her sweater, unbuckling the belt of her jeans. Rosemary thought, "It'll go wrong again. I can't stop thinking. Someone might be walking up here. I won't be able to let go." But the sun went on shining and the distant lark sang, high up in the blue air, and Rosemary found herself concerned only with her body and with Bran's, not caring what was happening beyond the thorn bushes. This, here and now, was what mattered. For the first time in her life she felt all in one piece, no division between mind and body, everything traveling towards one goal. No doubts and no uncertainties could stop her now.

"You might be right," Bran said into her hair.

From a long way away Rosemary heard and said, "What about?"

"The house."

She was too lazy, too drowsily content to question him anymore. She felt him roll to her side and knew that he was pulling her coat over them both. He had one arm under her and her head was against his shoulder. Drowned in comfort, she slept.

She woke twenty minutes later with the first shiver of cold. The day was still bright, but the warmth seemed to have left the sunlight. She sat up and looked at Bran, lying beside her with his eyes shut, his funny hair wildly tufted. He looked peaceful; much more peaceful than Bran, awake and alert, generally looked. When he was awake, Rosemary thought, his expressions changed so quickly, his face moved so much, it was difficult to tell what he really looked like.

Bran's eyes flew open and he sat up.

"Getting chilly."

"It is a bit."

"You were asleep," he said.

"Weren't you?"

"Not really." He stood up and held out a hand. "Come on. Can't have you catching cold." When she was standing beside him, he hugged her suddenly and kissed her. "Well? It was better next time, wasn't it?"

"It was for you too?" She didn't need to ask.

"And how!" He gave her another hug, then started walking briskly back towards the car. As they drove back down the unmade road, Rosemary shivered.

"You did get cold," Bran said, contrite.

"No I didn't. I'm beautifully warm. Feel." She put a hand against his cheek.

"What is it then?"

"It's silly."

"Be a devil. Be silly."

"I don't want to go back."

"The mist's cleared a bit. It's easier to see where we're going."

"It's not just the mist. It's the house."

He said, after a moment's silence, "We'll be together."

"That makes it better. Only . . ."

"Only what?"

"There is something about the house. It isn't just Veryan and me."

"She's a funny kid. Never met one her age who never said anything."

"I forgot!" Rosemary said suddenly.

"What?"

"She wanted me to tell you. Did you know her mother and father were killed in a car crash in January?"

Bran whistled through his teeth. "Christ! Are you sure?"

"She told me. She says Jamie won't talk about it."

"Why'd she tell you?"

"She wanted Philip to know."

"Why couldn't she tell him herself?"

"I don't think she likes him much. She said I could tell you too."

"Poor bloody kid! She must've had a time." He remembered the day when he'd caught her sitting among them with the book held in front of her and the tears

146

falling silently behind it. He remembered her nightmare and forgave her for what she'd done to his sex life. Easy to forgive that now.

"That's why she wears her dad's pullover," he said.

"Must be. I hadn't thought."

"When did she tell you?"

"Saturday. In the church."

"Poor kid," Bran said again.

"She is . . . funny, though. Not just because of that. She's really grown-up in some ways. She said Jamie wants to pretend it all hasn't happened, but she knew she couldn't do that. She said she had to stop being brave and let herself mind about it."

"That's it. She's real. Jamie isn't."

They had come to the crossroads. Bran locked the wheel around to the right, made a hairpin bend and they were back on the road to Winter's End.

"Is Philip real?"

"Not these last few days, he hasn't been. But not like Jamie and Cary. They're not real because they're putting on an act all the time. Philip's sort of unreal isn't putting on an act. . . ."

"What is it, then?"

"It's more like as if he wasn't real to himself. Or as if we weren't real to him. I don't know. I don't understand Philip. One minute he seems to have gone all soft and to let Cary do whatever she likes with him, the next he's getting het up about something that doesn't matter. This morning he was practically paranoid."

"What's paranoid?"

"Suspicious. Thinking everyone's plotting behind your back. That's how he was talking this morning, anyway."

The car swung off the road between the gateposts and up the drive. The mist had almost disappeared, but after the sunlight and the clarity of the hilltop, the drive was dark and shadowed. Against the evergreen conifers and the gray hill, the house gleamed, as delicate as if it were made of spun silver.

"It is beautiful. But I don't like it," Rosemary said.

"I'll look after you."

"I know. But . . ."

He was out of the car, opening the boot to get out the supplies they'd brought. As she went to help him, he slid a hand up her sleeve and touched the inside of her wrist.

"Rosey? Love me?"

She said, "Yes." But already the shadow of that spidery portico had fallen across her, and though her mind knew that the word was true, she missed the deep assurance that comes direct from the heart.

12

As soon as it got dark the mist returned. It seemed to Rosemary, going up to her room early in the evening to put on an extra pullover, that there was mist inside the house as well as out. In spite of the sun and the lovemaking that afternoon, she felt that the chilled atmosphere was penetrating her bones.

She was in her room with the sweater half pulled on over her head when there was a knock on her door. Her first thought was joyful. Bran! But it wasn't his knock, and when she said, "Come in," it was Veryan who obeyed her.

She came in and shut the door carefully behind her. She said, "I'm sorry to disturb you."

"That's all right." It wasn't. She was still annoyed

with Veryan. The girl stood just inside the closed door, looking at her with those extraordinary eyes.

"I think something bad is happening to Philip," she said.

"What do you mean, bad?"

"He's . . . strange."

Remembering how he'd taken the news about Veryan's parents and what Bran had said about him a few hours earlier, Rosemary couldn't deny this. She said, "He is, a bit."

"Not just a bit. There's something wrong."

"With Philip?"

"It's worse for him than for us."

"Because it's his house?" Rosemary hadn't known she was going to say this until it came out. She said quickly, "No, that's silly."

"I don't think it's silly," Veryan said.

"But what difference could the house make? I mean . . ." But the house did make a difference. She had felt it herself

"I don't know how it works. But it's making Philip different."

"Why don't you like him?" Rosemary asked. Veryan's eyes seemed to get even larger.

"Who said I didn't like him?"

"No one. I just thought you didn't."

Veryan didn't answer that for a minute. Then she said, "I love him."

"You *what*?"

"I've always loved him. I mean, ever since Jamie brought him home. That's more than a year ago."

Rosemary started to say, "But . . ." Veryan interrupted her.

"Don't say I'm too young. People always think you can't fall in love till you're sixteen or seventeen."

"I wasn't going to say that. I was going to say you can't know him very well."

"Do you have to know a person very well to fall in love with them?" Veryan asked.

Remembering her own hopeless pining for John Tarot, with whom she'd hardly exchanged a word, Rosemary could only say, "I suppose not."

"He's the only one of Jamie's friends who's ever talked to me. Really talked."

"What about?" Rosemary asked.

"Different things. Sometimes it's easier to talk to a person you don't know very well."

Rosemary nodded.

"It was like that. He talked and he listened."

"Does he know that you . . . that you're in love with him?"

"You won't tell him?"

"No, of course I shan't."

"Though I don't think he'd believe you if you did. Not now."

"Bran thinks there's something funny about him too," Rosemary said.

Veryan snatched at this. "Bran does? He's going to be a doctor isn't he?"

"He hasn't got on to seeing patients yet. I don't think . . ."

Veryan interrupted her. "But he's clever. What does

he think's wrong with Philip?"

"He said Philip seems to think everyone's plotting things against him. He said he didn't seem as if he was real to himself."

"That's it! He's not real. He's . . ." She hesitated. "It's like as if he was in a sort of dream. A bad dream."

"A nightmare? Like yours the other night?"

Veryan's answer was explicit. "Poor Philip, then."

Rosemary stared at her.

"Isn't there something we could do?" Veryan said.

"What? What could we do?"

"Couldn't we get him away?"

"You mean take him? Without asking?"

"Bran has his car," Veryan said.

"Cary might be able to persuade him," Rosemary said.

"Could you ask her? She wouldn't listen to me."

"Do you really think he'd be all right if he went away?"

Veryan had begun, "He won't be if he stays . . ." when she was cut short by a shout from the stairs. "Rosemary! Supper! Ve-ry-an!" As she opened her door, Rosemary heard Bran finish the summons with, "Hurry up. It's time and tide."

"What do you mean, time and tide?" she asked him as she reached the bottom of the stairs where he was waiting for them.

"Wait for no man. Soufflé, of course. Straight out of one of those women's magazines, it looks. Cary! Don't cut your masterpiece till the girls have seen it," he called as they went towards the kitchen.

"Where have you been?" Philip said to Rosemary directly she came into the room. The soufflé, perfect, its smooth brown crust just broken to show a creamy pale inside, stood on the table in front of Cary, who plunged a spoon in as he spoke.

"Upstairs getting a sweater. I was cold."

"You took a long time. What were you doing?" he asked Veryan.

"I had to go to the bathroom."

Philip didn't comment on this, but during the meal and afterwards Rosemary saw his eyes examining each of the others, staring at their faces as if he were trying to read their thoughts. Once when she looked at him their eyes met. Philip immediately looked away.

"He asks you where you've been like . . . like the Spanish Inquisition," she said to Bran that night. They were lying naked together in Rosemary's bed. Not, however, making love. What had decided this, Bran wasn't sure. Fear of failure? Preoccupation? He was astonished that he could lie so quietly beside Rosemary, his right side touching all the way down her left, his arm under her shoulders, her head against his shoulder. She had said, when he'd come, late, into her room, "Bran? Do you mind if . . . ?" He'd said, "Not if you don't want to," and discovered in himself relief instead of disappointment.

"That funny kid's right. What she said to you about him being in a dream."

"Do you think we ought to try to get him out of the house?"

"Might be a good idea to get him back to civilization

153

so there's a doctor handy if he needs one."

"There might be a doctor in the village."

"I don't believe Philip would agree to see him, even if there is," Bran said.

"But if he's really . . . ill?"

"D'you think he knows he's ill? I don't."

"No—o. I suppose he doesn't."

They considered this in silence for a time.

"Sleepy?" Bran asked.

"Not very."

"Worried?"

"Veryan made me feel as if something really bad might happen."

"Suppose Cary's right?" Bran said.

"What about?"

"Veryan. She could just be the kind of hysterical kid that goes around stirring up trouble."

"She's not like that," Rosemary said.

"Hope not. It's bad enough having Philip getting like this, without having a teenage hysteric to cope with as well."

"I don't think she's hysterical. I think she's right."

"Still doesn't solve the problem of what we're going to do."

"Couldn't you get him to go with you in the car and then just take him somewhere? To his home?"

"Kidnap him? He wouldn't stay in the car a minute once he saw what I was up to. And there'd be his kit and all that."

Rosemary said, "Yes," with a long sigh.

"Go to sleep, love. Something'll turn up."

"I hope it's something good."

There was a long silence. Bran, still fully awake, could feel tension gradually drain out of the body next to him. Her breathing grew light and shallow. She felt soft and defenseless beside him. When he pulled her closer with the arm under her body, she stirred and said, "Bran?"

"I'm here, Rosey."

"I'm glad you're here," she said and was asleep again.

After a time Bran slept too.

13

The mist had cleared the next morning, but there was no sun. The day was gray and chilly. By common unspoken consent they spent the morning in the kitchen, working or pretending to work. It wasn't just his imagination, Bran thought, that made him aware of an atmosphere of unease in the room. Several times when he looked up from the textbook which wasn't holding all his attention, he saw Cary's eyes still bent on the page which she hadn't turned all morning; saw Philip's gaze flickering from one of his companions to another. Jamie, always the most restless of the party, yawned and stretched and looked out of the window, opened his mouth as if he were going to speak, then ostentatiously checked himself. Rosemary read steadily, but Bran saw how often she looked around the room, and then towards him for reassurance. Veryan held a book in her lap, but she spent more time considering the others with that serious, reticent stare of hers than she did in reading. Bran, observing how long her eyes rested on Philip, wondered what she'd thought she meant when she'd told Rosey that she loved Philip. A schoolgirl crush? A romantic fantasy? Neither seemed to suit Veryan. Peculiar kid.

It was nearly midday when Philip got up from the table and left the kitchen. He'd hardly shut the door behind him when Cary said in a voice just above a whisper, speaking to no one in particular, "Someone's got to help me."

"Help you how?" Bran said.

"It's Phil. He's gone absolutely around the bend. Last night he wouldn't let me sleep hardly at all. He talked all the time. . . ."

"What about?"

"He's mad. I told you, he said he couldn't work because of what I was thinking. Things like that."

"Must have been joking," Jamie said.

"He wasn't. He really meant it. He says we're all against him. Plotting. When I tried to get out of the room, he wouldn't let me go. He said I'd got to stay and listen."

"How d'you mean, he wouldn't let you go?"

"Locked the door and hid the key somewhere."

"He let you out this morning all right, did he?" Bran asked.

"He wasn't so bad this morning. He'd be furious if he

knew I'd told you though."

"He'll be back in a minute," Rosemary said, hearing the distant sound of the lavatory cistern.

"Can't you do something?" Cary appealed to Bran.

"We'd better try to get him back home as soon as possible," Bran said.

"I don't think he'd go. He thinks we're all trying . . ."

The door opened and Philip came in. He said, "You're talking about me." His voice was high and accusatory. He looked both angry and frightened.

Bran thought, "Cary's right. He is crazy." Aloud he said, "We were discussing what we'd do this afternoon." It was unfortunate that at the same moment Jamie said, "Of course we weren't. We were just saying what terrible weather . . ."

"I heard you," Philip said flatly.

No one answered this immediately.

Then Bran said, "You don't look well, that's all. Cary's worried about you."

"Cary's worried because she knows that I know."

"What do you know?"

"I know that you're all against me." He sat at the table and looked around at them.

"That's ridiculous! Why should we be against you?" Jamie said.

"You think you can get me out of this house. That's what you were planning just now. You won't, you know. I'm staying here."

"We're all leaving on Saturday," Cary said.

"The others may be. I'm not."

Jamie made the mistake of looking towards Bran. Philip, intercepting the look, said immediately, "You're planning something behind my back. I know you are."

"Cool it! All we're saying is that we've got to get away at the end of the week. If you don't want to come with us, that's your affair," Bran said. He hoped he'd sounded adult, reasonable. It wasn't how he felt.

"Not Cary. She's mine." He put a hand on Cary's arm. Rosemary saw her shudder.

"Saturday's a long way off. Let's leave it and see how Cary feels then. And you," Bran said.

"Cary's not going."

Cary looked at them around the table. Her eyes said, "Don't leave me! I'm frightened!" Bran said, "We don't need to decide anything now."

"You don't decide. I decide," Philip said.

"We all decide together. And now let's decide to shut up and get some work done," Bran said. He was surprised that Philip appeared to accept this, although during the next hour nobody did much work. Nobody spoke, either. It wasn't until after lunch, when the plates and mugs were being cleared away, that Philip said suddenly, "So what did you decide?"

"Decide about what?" Bran asked.

"You said you'd been discussing what to do this afternoon." He sounded accusing, as if he'd caught them in a conspiracy.

"I'll have to go down to the village for supplies," Bran said

"I'll come too," Cary said at once.

"You went the other day," Philip said.

"There's no law against going there twice, is there?" Cary asked.

"What are you going to buy?"

"I need a nail file. I left mine at home," Cary said.

"You're not going," Philip said to her.

"Why not?"

"I want you here."

"I'll take Rosemary and Veryan," Bran said.

"I'll come along too, if you don't mind. There are one or two things I could be doing with," Jamie said elaborately casual.

Rosemary saw Cary look around the table in a terrified appeal. Jamie couldn't have missed it, and she waited for him to say he'd changed his mind, he'd stay. But Jamie avoided her eye and said nothing. Rosemary said to Bran, "There's nothing I need to go to the village for. I'll stay here." She saw Cary's flash of relief and hoped Bran would understand.

Veryan said, "I'm not going either."

Bran asked, "Are you sure?"

"I'm sure, thank you."

"Why don't you come with us?" Bran said to Philip.

"I told you. I'm not leaving this house."

"Just as you like." Bran tried for a convincingly casual voice. He said to Rosemary, "Come and open the garage for me," and pushed her out of the kitchen in front of him, without waiting for Philip to raise objections. As soon as they were out in the open air, she said, "Bran? I couldn't leave Cary here alone with . . ."

160

"I know. That bloody Jamie! I'd have told him he'd got to stay if I hadn't thought it'd make Philip worse."

"What are you going to do in the village?"

"Find a doctor. If I can."

"You don't think Philip's dangerous, do you?"

"I just don't know," Bran said.

"What shall we do?"

"Keep him quiet. It doesn't matter how many lies you have to tell him. Humor him. Don't talk to each other except about ordinary things out loud in front of him, so he can't think you're plotting against him. I'll get back as quickly as I can."

"I wish you hadn't got to go."

"So do I. But what the hell can I do? If I knew the name of a local doctor I'd have tried to phone him, but as I don't, the only thing is to go down to the village to find out."

They reached the garage. Rosemary held the door which would swing shut, while Bran started up the engine and maneuvered the car out onto the drive. She was shutting the door again when Jamie came out of the house, opened the passenger door, and got in beside Bran.

"Why the hell did you want to come with me? You ought to have stayed with Cary," Bran said, furious.

"With Philip in that mood? I wouldn't have a chance to get anywhere near her," Jamie said.

"I'm not talking about make yourself agreeable. She needs someone with her. She's terrified."

"Why didn't you stay, then?"

"I've got to get a doctor. There's something wrong with Philip. God knows what. That's what I'm going to the village for. What did you think it was? To get a couple of stamps?"

Rosemary came to the car and asked, "Anything wrong?"

"Do you want me to stay, then?" Jamie asked Bran.

"There's Philip coming out of the house now," Rosemary said.

"No. We can't change now. You wouldn't be any more use than a sick headache, anyway," Bran said. He let in the clutch. To Rosemary he said, " 'Bye, Rosey. Keep it cool." As he drove towards the road beyond the dark shrubs, he worried. This was what total responsibility was like then. Why had he ever thought he wanted to be a doctor?

"You're driving too fast," Jamie said.

"I want to get back as soon as I can. I don't like leaving those girls there with Philip."

"Old Philip'd never hurt anyone. Gentle as a lamb," Jamie said.

"Is that why you were so anxious to get away?"

Short silence. Then Jamie said, "There's that old woman."

"Which old woman?"

"She came up to clean around the house last week."

Bran saw her now. A small, scurrying figure coming up the road towards them.

"Hope she's not going up to the house. That'd really put the lid on it," Bran said.

"She'd be somebody else with the girls. You said you

didn't like them being there by themselves," Jamie said.

"You can't be that stupid!" Bran said, driving faster than ever. Jamie relapsed into a sulky silence which lasted until they were in the village street.

Bran made directly for Nancy Rammage, and was grateful that there was no one else in the shop.

"Trouble? It's Mr. Philip, isn't it?" she said at once.

"How did you know?"

"The family's been there a good while."

"You mean . . . something inherited?"

"Not like you mean. Only when they come to live up there."

"This place?"

She said, "The house." She added quickly, "Mind you there's people'll tell you it's nothing but talk."

"But how could a house . . . ?"

She cut him short. "How is it taking him? Mr. Philip?"

"I've got to find a doctor. Is there one here? In the village?"

"Dr. Fellows, over at Temple Lacey. He's the nearest. But he'll be over at the hospital this afternoon."

"Where's the hospital?"

"That's in Englesham. Twenty miles off."

Twenty miles. That meant at least half an hour there and another half hour back. Bran said, "Thanks," and went back to the car.

"What . . . ?" Jamie began, but Bran didn't wait to answer. He got behind the wheel and drove towards the scarlet telephone kiosk by the bus station.

"What . . . ?" Jamie began again. Bran stopped

him with, "I'm going to try ringing the local hospital. And Rosemary, if I can get through."

He was out of luck with the hospital. The girl at the switchboard couldn't page Dr. Fellows unless it was for an urgent call from another doctor. She could take a message and ask Dr. Fellows to ring back. Bran groaned. He couldn't risk the call coming through up at the house before he got back. He thanked her and hung up, despairing. He dialed the Winter's End number. The bell rang two, three, four times, and then to his relief he heard Rosemary's voice.

"Rosey? It's me. Bran. How's everything?"

"All right. I think. Where are you?"

"In the village. What's happening? Just answer yes or no if it's awkward. Is Philip in the room with you?"

"No. He's upstairs. Cary told him he ought to go and have a rest this afternoon . . ."

"That's fine. Then . . ."

". . . only he made her go with him."

"She all right?"

"I don't know. She didn't want to go. She said . . ."

"What?"

"I can't tell you just now."

Bran didn't know what she meant. "Look, love. I'll have to go over to Englesham. There's a hospital there and the doctor's in it. It'll take an hour or a bit more to get there and back."

He heard the dismay in her voice as she repeated, "More than an hour?"

"I've got to get hold of a doctor, Rosey."

"Yes."

"Think you'll be all right?"

"I expect we will. Only . . . Bran . . ."

"I'll get back as quick as I can. Love you."

She said, "I do too." That was the only bit of comfort he could get that afternoon.

14

In Winter's End, Rosemary put down the receiver and looked around the hall. No one there. No one to be seen on the corridor that ran around the staircase on the upper floor. Why did she have the feeling that everything she did was watched, everything she said overheard? The house? If walls have ears at least they haven't tongues so that they can pass on what they know. And somewhere around the place was Mrs. Eye, slipping from room to room and making no more noise than a crooked shadow. She'd arrived ten minutes after Bran and Jamie had driven off. As Bran had said, it put the final edge to her discomfort.

"Just popped in to see that everything's all right," she'd said as she'd done on the first occasion. Rosemary, anxious to get rid of her as quickly as possible, said, "Yes, thank you. Everything's fine."

"Only the two of you here, then?" Mrs. Eye said. Her little eyes darted about her as if she might find the others in hiding somewhere about the kitchen, where Rosemary and Veryan were alone.

"The others are upstairs." Rosemary didn't want to betray the fact that Bran and Jamie were not in the house.

"I saw two of them go along the road in the car. Gone to the village, have they?"

"They'll be back soon," Rosemary said hopefully.

"I'll go up and get their rooms done first, then."

"But . . . it was only Friday when you did them before."

"I like to keep the place looking nice," Mrs. Eye said.

"We shan't be here much longer. It's hardly worthwhile . . ."

"It's not your place, is it? So I don't see it's for you to say what's to be done and what isn't. I've always kept the house as it should be, and I'm not giving up now." She gave Rosemary a malevolent stare and disappeared.

"I wish she wasn't here," Veryan said under her breath.

"I couldn't prevent her coming in. Could I?"

"She'd have come whatever you said," Veryan answered.

They listened. Silence.

"She won't be able to get into Cary and Philip's room," Rosemary said.

"Will she try?"

"I don't know." Rosemary thought uncomfortably of the scene that she and Veryan had unwillingly witnessed immediately after Bran and Jamie had left. She'd come back into the house, wishing that it was her out there in the car with Bran, wishing she didn't have to go back inside. Philip had held the front door open for her. When he'd shut it behind her, she'd felt as if he were closing the gates of a prison.

They'd gone back into the kitchen, where Cary and Veryan were clearing the draining board of the washed dishes. Philip sat in a chair and looked on. His eyes followed Cary as she moved about, and Rosemary thought, "That's what people in torment must look like." She saw too that Cary was uneasily conscious of the watch kept on her, and that it made her uncharacteristically clumsy. A white-and-gold saucer they'd used as a butter dish slipped from her fingers and fell into the washing-up bowl. Philip exclaimed and Cary started.

"Why can't you be more careful?" Philip said sharply

"It's isn't broken. Look!" She held it up to show.

"You might have broken it."

Rosemary thought of what Bran had said. Humor him, keep it cool. She said to Philip, "Cary's tired. I'll put away the rest of the things."

"I'm tired too," Philip said

"Didn't you sleep well last night?" She'd asked it before she'd remembered Cary's saying that he'd been talking most of the night.

"Not proper sleep. Not the right kind of sleep."

168

She didn't want to ask what he meant in case this provoked another outburst. She said, "Why don't you sleep this afternoon, then? It might make you feel better."

"Better than what?" He was suspicious again.

"Not so tired."

"Do you think I'd have the right sort of sleep this afternoon?" he asked her.

"You could try," Rosemary said, without knowing what he meant. She was relieved when he stood up and said, "All right. I'll go and try." Before she'd had time to congratulate herself on the success of her maneuver, he added, "But Cary's got to come too."

"No! I don't . . ." Cary began.

"Just to come up to our room. Then you can come down again."

"I don't want to go upstairs," Cary said.

"Then I won't go either."

Silence. Rosemary didn't know what to do next. She said to Cary, "Why not just go to the top of the stairs with Philip? It wouldn't hurt you." Cary hesitated, then apparently made up her mind that it was the lesser evil. She said, "All right. I'll come and see you to the door."

Rosemary and Veryan heard their footsteps die away on the stairs. Then the sudden slam of a door. Two minutes later Cary had still not returned.

"He tricked her inside," Veryan said.

"Do you think she'll be all right? Suppose he . . ." She didn't know what she feared.

"She'll be all right as long as she doesn't frighten him more."

"More?"

"More than he is already."

"What's he frightened of?" Rosemary asked.

"He thinks we're all his enemies."

"Perhaps he'll go to sleep."

"Cary can't give him the right sort of sleep."

"What do you mean by the right sort? What was Philip talking about?"

"Don't you know?" Veryan asked. She slightly emphasized the pronoun. Rosemary opened her mouth to say no, then shut it again. She did know. The short sleep she'd had on Bran's shoulder up on the hillside the afternoon before had been different from the sleep she had here in this house. How different? She could only think of words that seemed stupid. Her sleep here was thin. It wasn't that she woke during the night or that she had bad dreams. But compared to that quarter of an hour of golden sleep yesterday, it was poor. Impoverished. Gray. She found the improbable word "empty" in her mind, and she repeated it aloud. "Empty. Empty sleep. Is that what Philip means?"

It was at this moment that Mrs. Eye had sidled into the kitchen, immeasurably increasing Rosemary's discomfort. Knowing that she was somewhere about in the house, listening at keyholes, spying out the land, made it nearly impossible to sit still and quite impossible to concentrate. After an uneasy quarter of an hour of pretending to read, she said, "I wish Bran and Jamie would come back."

"They might be back any minute now," Veryan said.

"If there's a doctor in Winter Lacey."

"What would a doctor do for Philip?"

"He'd tell us what to do. He might give him tranquilizers. Or something. Something to make him sleep."

"Real sleep?"

"Why did you say Cary couldn't give it to him?"

"She's too unhappy with herself," Veryan said.

"Cary is? You mean now?"

"She's an unhappy person."

"But . . . !" Rosemary thought of Cary's beauty, of her brains, of her instant appeal to the opposite sex. She'd always assumed that Cary had everything that she, Rosemary, would have liked for herself.

"She'd have to know who she really is, to give Philip anything," Veryan said.

"Doesn't she know?"

"She doesn't know what other people are like, either. Jamie's the same. He's always trying to make people believe he's the sort of person he'd like to be, so he doesn't have time to see what they're thinking."

"Is that why you said she couldn't get Philip to sleep properly?"

"How could you help someone you don't know?" Veryan said.

"Could you?" Rosemary asked.

"I could try. But I don't think he'd believe that I could. He'd think I was too young."

"Too young to help him?"

"Too young to love," Veryan said.

"You're only five years younger than he is."

"It's a long five years," Veryan said.

"It won't seem as much when you're older," Rosemary said.

"He'll have found someone else by then. He might wait for me if I could go to bed with him now. But he wouldn't."

"But . . . I mean. You're terribly young for that."

"Lot of girls my age do. Not always because of loving, though. And often it doesn't work."

Taken aback, Rosemary said, "How do you know?"

Veryan said, "I haven't tried it. So I suppose I don't, really. It's just that I do love Philip. Properly. I wouldn't mind going to bed with him because it'd be right for me. But it wouldn't be for him. Not if he was thinking all the time that I'm too young."

She turned those dark-river eyes on Rosemary. "Do you love Bran?"

"I think so."

"I think he loves you too. You're lucky."

The telephone shrilled. Rosemary went to answer it. She came back to the kitchen and said, "Bran's going to Englesham. To the hospital. He says it'll take more than an hour before he's back. He asked if we were all right."

"Did you say we were?"

"Mm. But I said to come back soon."

Silence.

"If anything went wrong, Cary would call out. Wouldn't she?" Rosemary said.

"I can't hear anything," Veryan said.

"I can't either."

172

"I wish that that Mrs. Eye wasn't here."

"So do I," Rosemary said with feeling.

Silence again. The enveloping quiet of the house wrapped them in fear.

15

By a combination of exaggeration and persuasion, Bran got the elderly man at the hospital's reception desk to page Dr. Fellows and bring him to a telephone. Bran leaned over the polished wood desk and heard a voice ask irritably, "Who is it? I'm in the middle of a ward round."

"It's Philip Edmund from Winter's End, Winter Lacey."

There was a second's pause. "I don't know any Philip Edmund."

"He's the nephew of Peter Edmund. He's . . . ."

"I thought you said you were Philip Edmund," the voice said, sharp and hurried.

"It's about him. I'm a friend of his. We've been staying at the house with him. . . ."

"What's wrong? Simmonds said it was an emergency. Accident?"

"I think he's a bit crazy," Bran said.

"What sort of crazy? Violent? Suicidal?"

"I don't know. We none of us know how bad he is. We've got three girls with us, and they're frightened."

A long, exasperated sigh came over the wire, then the voice said, "You're in reception, aren't you? I'll come down for five minutes."

Dr. Fellows was sixtyish, with a head of fine straight silver hair and a deeply wrinkled face. He wasted no time in preliminaries. Sitting on one of the wooden benches in the waiting room, he said to Bran and Jamie, "Which of you was I talking to just now?"

"Me," Bran said.

"Tell me, then. How old is this boy?"

"Nineteen. He's first year at university. We all are."

"You said he's been behaving oddly. How?"

"He gets excited. Ordinarily he's not an excitable chap. Last night he wouldn't let his girl friend sleep, talked all night. She's frightened. . . ."

"He hasn't attacked her? Or threatened her in any way?"

"No."

"Is he depressed? Miserable? Does he cry? Is he retarded . . . slow in his reactions?"

"No. But he's suspicious."

"Suspicious of who?"

"Of all of us. He seems to think we're trying to get

him out of the house. It does belong to him. But of course we aren't."

"You say he's Peter Edmund's nephew?"

Bran asked, "Is there something he could have inherited?"

Dr. Fellows fixed him with a sharp blue eye.

"People inherit tendencies more than full-blown psychoses. There are one or two carried in the genes, but there's nothing like that in the Edmunds. Why d'you ask?"

"I'm not sure. I suppose . . . People in the village . . . they don't exactly say anything. It's more the way they ask. If we're all right up at the house. As if they expected something to happen. . . ."

"Was that what started the boy off?"

"I don't think he heard much of it."

"Where is he now?"

"In the house. With the three girls."

"You've got a car? Could you bring him here?"

"He won't go anywhere. He won't leave the house at all."

The blue eye was turned on Bran again.

"Do you personally think he's bad enough for me to send an ambulance over? As far as you can judge?"

Jamie began, "He really ought . . ."

Bran said, "I just don't know."

"You said the girl was frightened?"

"Yes, but . . ." He didn't know how to explain that Cary was the sort of girl who would be frightened by anything she didn't understand.

"Trouble is, we're short staffed. Like everybody else.

It's twenty-five miles from here to the house. Might be another two or three hours before an ambulance got there. I think the best thing is for me to come over and have a look at this young man of yours when I finish here. If you think you can hold on that long."

"That'd be fantastic. When . . . ?"

"Can't get away for another hour. Probably not then. Might not be before six or seven this evening. Think you can manage?"

"We'll try," Bran said.

"If you think he's worse—any question of violence against any of you, or if he starts talking about doing away with himself—ring me here. I'll leave a message you're to be put straight through. All right?"

"That's great! It's really good of you. . . ."

"Known the family a long time. See you," Dr. Fellows said and went, fast, along the green-and-dark-brown corridor. The moment he was out of earshot, Jamie said, "You ought to have insisted on them sending someone over with us."

"If you felt so strongly, why didn't you tell him yourself?"

"I don't know anything about illness. Especially not mental illness," Jamie said.

"I don't, either. Only someone's got to make up their mind."

As they got back into the mini Jamie said, "Mind you, I don't suppose he's dangerous. I was just thinking that he ought to have treatment as soon as we can get it to him."

"You needn't trouble to explain."

"What d'you mean?" Jamie said, aggrieved.

"Sure, you were only thinking about Philip. Like you're only thinking about Veryan when you try to make her pretend your parents are still alive." He hadn't meant to say it. He wouldn't have come out with it like that if he hadn't been strung up and anxious and intolerably annoyed. There was a short silence.

"How did you know?" Jamie asked.

"Veryan told Rosemary."

"Everyone says it's bad to brood," Jamie said.

"Hasn't anyone ever told you it's bad to bottle up? Anyway, why do you have to be told? Don't you know, yourself, what's good or bad for you?"

Jamie didn't answer. Bran, squinting sideways, saw his face set.

He said, "What happened to your parents? I just know it was a road accident."

"It was a pileup on the M 6. Foggy. It wasn't Dad's fault. He was a really good driver."

"You can't always get out of the way of bloody fools driving too fast when they can't see anything."

"They said it was instantaneous. . . ."

"How did you hear?"

"My aunt came up. The same day. Trouble was . . ."

"What?" Bran asked. Not because he was interested in Jamie's aunt, but because it was obvious that now he'd begun, Jamie needed to talk.

"I've never liked her much. She's not really an aunt, a sort of cousin, really. When I got the message she was there, I felt . . . I kept her waiting for a bit. I thought she'd just dropped in."

Bran could imagine it. The unwilling Jamie. The un-welcome cousin with the unbelievable news to impart. He said, "Must've been terrible."

Jamie said, in a voice which wasn't recognizably his, "I didn't believe it at first."

"Like—this couldn't happen to me?"

"That's right. Wouldn't have been so bad if I'd . . . If we'd . . . I mean. It's easier for Veryan. She hadn't ever got across them like I did. You know how it is."

"Needing to shoot down their ideas so as to show you don't have to agree with everything they've said?"

"That's it! Not my mother so much. But my father . . . We used to have fights. . . ."

"Everyone does," Bran said. There'd been evenings when he and his own dad had sat shouting at each other across the supper table. What had it been about? Im-migration? The common market? Alice over the hill? He couldn't even remember now. But then his dad had stayed alive and well to disagree with another day. Jamie's had been cut off suddenly. Unhouseled, disap-pointed, unaneled. Of course. It wasn't because he'd been killed without the chance to make his peace with God that old Hamlet was griping about his sudden death. It was because he'd died before he'd had a chance to make peace with his son. Young Hamlet and old Hamlet had had an almighty row and young Hamlet had gone post-ing off to Wittenberg in a rage, and while he was away old Hamlet had died. Young Hamlet had felt just as bad about it as his father. Or worse. It wasn't his uncle, remorseless, treacherous, lecherous, kindless villain, he was ranting at. It was himself.

Poor Jamie.

He said again, "Everyone does. If you didn't fight, how'd you know who you were? Your dad probably wanted you to stand up to him. My dad says it's bloody awful having kids that tell you what you're doing wrong all the time, but it'd be worse if they didn't." This wasn't precisely what his dad had said, but it was right in essence.

"It used to upset my mother," Jamie said.

There was a silence. Bran drove as fast as he dared. His mind had gone back to Rosey. He was wondering what she was doing now. Yesterday afternoon at about this time, they'd just about got back from the hillside. It had been good. Very good. Of course she was unpracticed, she'd been hesitant, but not a tease, not a prude. She would learn quickly.

He'd almost forgotten Jamie when a slight sound made him glance quickly away from the road and then immediately back again. It wouldn't do to let on that he'd seen that Jamie, at last, was mourning for his dead.

16

It seemed that they'd been sitting in the kitchen for hours, though it was really not more than twenty or thirty minutes. Suddenly Rosemary said, "Cary!" and made for the door.

The cold silence had been broken. Upstairs someone was beating with fists against a door.

Out in the hall, Rosemary stopped. In the corridor above, the beating on the door was accompanied by words, spoken in a sort of screaming whisper more horrifying than a shout. She heard, "Disgusting! I know what you're doing in there! In the daytime! Filthy beasts . . ." The whisper died away and was drowned by a new, more violent assault on the door. Rosemary rounded the curve of the stairs and saw Mrs. Eye like a demented insect, arms flailing against the door of Cary and Philip's room, a stream of half-heard abuse coming from a throat tight with rage.

Rosemary called out, "Stop!" Her voice echoed around the well of the staircase and up into the glass dome. It came back to her like a mockery.

She hardly expected that she'd be heard or, if heard, obeyed. She was astonished when the battering fists dropped and the obscene torrent of words was halted in midflow. Astonishing too, and frightening, was the immediate change in Mrs. Eye. In a moment she'd become the apparently harmless little woman whose business it was to keep the house clean and tidy. She was saying, ". . . Seems like the door's stuck. I can't get it open to go in and see to the room." With her eyes she dared Rosemary to accuse her.

"Cary's in there. She was trying to get some sleep."

"And where's Mr. Philip?"

Behind her Rosemary heard a deep breath. Veryan. Strengthened by this knowledge, she said, "I don't see that it's your business where he is." She found that fear and rage together made her tremble as she spoke.

"It's my business to see that this house is kept as it should be. Now that it's Mr. Philip's, it's him I take my orders from. Not from you!" She spat this out with a venomed malice that hit Rosemary like a physical blow. Before she could answer, Mrs. Eye, with one of the darting movements, had scuttled towards the door leading to the deserted wing and had disappeared. They heard her footsteps in the uncarpeted passage beyond.

182

"D'you think she's going?" Veryan breathed and was answered in the same moment by the click of the lock and the faint whine of the hinges of the back door.

Veryan said, "Philip!" At the same time Rosemary's mind said, "Cary!" She ran up the remaining steps and along the corridor to the closed door. Veryan remained by the stair head, watching intently.

There was no sound from behind the door.

Rosemary tapped lightly. Nails rather than fingers. She called softly, "Cary? It's me. Rosemary. Are you . . . all right?"

The silence was total. No one spoke. No one moved. The pale walls and the icy dome overhead glittered in the early dusk. The house felt like a mausoleum, a house for the dead.

"Cary! Please say something! What's happening?" Repeated, useless words. She couldn't find any others. She didn't know what dark imaginings were forcing her to invade the privacy of Philip, whom she didn't love, and of Cary, whom she didn't like. She knew only that if anything was to be done now it must be done by herself. Veryan was too young. Philip was too much disturbed. Cary? Cary was most in danger. She said again, more urgently, "Cary! It's Rosemary. Cary!"

No answer. Silence in the room. Silence all around. Inside her head Rosemary heard Mrs. Eye's hoarse invective of abuse and wondered how much had penetrated the door to those two inside the room. She thought, "If she'd seen Bran and me yesterday!" She felt sick at the idea. So what was Cary feeling? What was she doing?

She raged against her own powerlessness. Against that locked door she could do nothing. She could only say over and over again, "Cary!" like a cry. A cry which nobody heard.

Veryan came and stood beside her. She said, "Let me."

"They're not listening. You can't . . ."

"I could try."

"Go on, then."

Veryan stood as close to the door as Rosemary had done. But instead of saying Cary's name, she said the other. She said, "Philip!" Softly. Rosemary realized that she'd never before heard Veryan address Philip by name. She knew now from the way in which Veryan pronounced it that she was right. She did love him.

Another long silence.

"Philip!"

Why did Rosemary have the impression that she was not the only person listening? There is no difference between one absolute silence and another. As far as she could tell there had been no sound beyond the door.

"Philip!"

To know a person's name is to have power over them. That is why newborn babies, hundreds of years ago, were not taken out of the house until they had been christened. To be named for the Christian God. After that they were proof against being snatched by the fairies; or by more malevolent powers. In some primitive tribes the incest taboo requires that a brother never speak his sister's given name, nor she his. All this ran through Rosemary's mind, taking no time at all, in the renewed hush that followed Veryan's last invocation of Philip's name. Mrs. Eye hadn't used names at all, she thought. She hadn't granted Philip and Cary the dignity of named human beings—she'd addressed them like animals. She, Rosemary herself, had called imploringly to Cary. It was Veryan who had spoken Philip's name, with respect. And, yes. With love.

There was at last a sound. The key grated in the lock. The heavy door opened. Philip, wrapped in a blanket, blocked the doorway. The window shades had been drawn down over the windows and it was impossible to see anything in the shadowy room behind him.

He looked uncertainly at Veryan and Rosemary.

"Someone called me."

"I called you," Veryan said.

His eyes examined her. He said, "Why did you call me?"

Veryan said, "You have to come out."

"Out? Out where?"

"Out of the house."

Rosemary saw him stiffen, saw suspicion inform his searching look. He said, "They want to get me out of the house." She heard Veryan's serene reply: "You know I'm not your enemy."

Philip looked at her again, and Veryan returned the look. They faced each other like two adversaries, each assessing the other's resources, weaknesses, strengths. Philip said, "But you want me to leave the house," and Veryan answered, "It's making you ill."

"I'm not ill. Am I?" he asked her.

"Yes. You are ill."

He put a hand to his head. "Here?"

She put a hand on her own heart. "And here."

He said suddenly, in a sort of rage, "You don't know anything. You're only a kid." And with a barely perceptible trembling of the voice, Veryan said, "That's why you can believe me."

They confronted each other for a full half minute longer, Philip's eyes raking her face, searching for a sign of weakness or falsity, Veryan's eyes steady. Then Philip sighed. It was a long sigh, half a groan, the sound of the fatigue that lay like a dead weight over his whole face. It was the sound of despair or relief, impossible to tell which.

He said, like a child to a parent, asking for the instructions that it would obey, "Where shall I go to?"

"First put on your clothes," Veryan said.

He turned back into the room.

"Let Cary come out now," she said after him, and without looking around, Philip repeated after her, "Cary can come out now."

There was a rustle in the shadowed room behind him, and Cary came through the door. Not a Cary that Rosemary had ever seen before. Her hair hung in sodden strands around her swollen, red-eyed face. She too clutched a blanket around her, and blundered out into the corridor as if she couldn't see for the tears that ran down her cheeks. Rosemary put out a hand to steady her, and Cary caught it and held it as to a lifesaver. To her own surprise Rosemary put an arm round her. She said, "It's all right, Cary. You're all right." She felt Cary shiver violently, and the hand clasping hers was marble cold. She said, "We'll go down to the kitchen. It's warmer there." Veryan, standing by the door, said, "I'll wait for Philip."

Downstairs Rosemary made hot sweet tea, while Cary sat by the stove. She didn't speak at first; every now and then her body was shaken by something between a shudder and a sob. When she'd brought her the tea, Rosemary could hear Cary's teeth chattering on the mug. She wondered if she'd ever be able to get her warm again. She brought a second mug of tea and pulled the woolen rug over to put under Cary's icy feet. She took her coat off the hook by the back door and put it over Cary's knees. There was another long shiver, and then, in a curiously small voice, Cary said, "It was cold."

"You'll soon warm up now," Rosemary said.

"All my clothes are up there," Cary said.

"We could go up and get them as soon as Philip's . . ."

Cary cried out, "No! I'm not going back."

"When he's not there."

"No! I don't want ever . . . It was horrible. He's crazy. He wanted . . ." She shuddered again. "You don't know. I've never been with anyone . . . I thought I'd never get away from him." Her eyes overflowed again and she let the tears splash onto her hands holding the mug of tea.

Rosemary said, "Poor Cary," and thought how extraordinary that she should be able not only to say it but really to feel the sorrow too.

Cary asked presently, "What was all that screaming? It wasn't you, or . . . ?"

"It was that horrible little woman. Mrs. Eye."

"What did she want?"

Rosemary, embarrassed, said, "I thought . . . I think she thought . . . that you and Philip . . . might be making love. . . ."

Cary said, "Love!" on a rising sob. She looked away from Rosemary, and she shuddered.

"Bran and Jamie might be back any minute now," Rosemary said, to reassure herself as much as Cary.

Cary took long swallows of the tea. She said, "They've been away a long time."

"It's only about two hours."

"It feels longer."

"I hope Veryan's all right," Rosemary said.

"Veryan?"

"She's up there with Philip." Misgivings invaded her mind. She'd been persuaded by Veryan's certainty to leave her alone for . . . what? Ten minutes which might stretch for her into the infinity of endurance from which Cary had just escaped. She said, "I must go up and see what's happening." She was unprepared for the degree of dependence with which Cary cried out, "Don't leave me!"

"But . . . suppose he . . . If she can't manage . . . ?"

"He listened to her. Didn't he? When she called out to him."

"But . . ."

"He wouldn't do anything to her. She's only a kid."

It was what Philip had said. It was what Veryan had acquiesced in. It was also what made Rosemary say, "That's why I'm worried." She left Cary in the warm kitchen and went up the stairs.

The door of Philip's room stood open. That was a relief. Veryan was no longer on the watch outside it. Rosemary approached the door cautiously. She looked inside. But the dim room was quiet and it was empty. The bedclothes were tumbled, trailing over the floor. No sign of Philip or of Veryan. Rosemary looked around the room and gathered up an armful of Cary's clothes and, on her way back to the kitchen, looked in at each of the other bedrooms. Each was as deserted as the other. Downstairs again she said, "They've gone."

"Not there?" Cary asked.

"I didn't hear them go out. Did you?" Rosemary said.

"No." Cary began to dress, and almost at once she looked more like herself. She borrowed a comb from Rosemary and looked at herself critically in the small, round mirror hanging near the back door. Rosemary's eyes watched her, her attention almost entirely elsewhere. Into the mirror, Cary asked her reflection, "What's the matter?"

"I can't think where Veryan and Philip could have gone."

"They might have gone down into the village."

"What would they do there?"

"P'r'aps they thought they'd meet Jamie and Bran."

"I think we ought to go and look for them."

"I haven't got any shoes," Cary said.

"We ought to make sure they're not anywhere in the house. I only looked upstairs."

She left Cary in the kitchen and started the search. The big rooms on the ground floor were chillingly cold and dim. There were already dark shadows in corners and around the larger pieces of furniture. Rosemary was grateful that she didn't have to go right into any of the rooms. It was enough to open each door and to call Veryan's name, but even so the emptiness and the silence oppressed her. She felt like an intruder and, as if in apology for being the only living thing there, she found she was unconsciously treading more softly and lowering her voice to match the dead silence of those long-deserted rooms.

She had reached the last but one when she heard the sound of wheels on the gravel of the drive. Before she could reach the front door it had been flung open by Bran, and he was asking, "Is everything all right?" at the same moment as she said, "Did you see them? On the way here from the village?"

"See who? Philip . . . ?"

"And Veryan. They've gone. . . ."

"You mean he took her off? Why the hell . . . ?"

"He didn't take her, it'd have been her taking him. At least . . ."

Bran took her by the shoulders and shook her gently. "Calm down, love. Let's get out of this bloody mausoleum and sit down somewhere warm. Shut the door, damn you!" he shouted at Jamie. Then, as they went into the kitchen, he said again, "You're all right, are you?" to both Rosemary and Cary.

"We're all right. But Veryan . . ."

"What's Veryan got to do with Philip? Why did you let her go off with him?"

"It wasn't like that. He wouldn't listen to anyone else. . . ."

"You mean you think she told him to go out? She must be as crazy as he is."

"You know how he was about leaving the house? First of all she got him to open the door of his room and then she said he'd have to get out of the house. Only I didn't think she meant at once, I thought she'd wait till you got back. . . ."

"Where the hell could they have gone?"

"Cary thought they might have gone towards the village so as to meet you."

"We didn't see a soul. Do you know where she could have gone?" Bran demanded of Jamie.

"Of course I don't. She doesn't know this part of the country at all. She's only been out once or twice since we came. . . ."

Rosemary exclaimed.

"Thought of something?"

"She did go out. On Saturday. I met her . . ."

"Where?"

"In the churchyard. D'you think . . . ?"

"Why would she want to take Philip to the churchyard?" Jamie said. Rosemary saw Bran's quick look at

Jamie before he said, "Don't know why she might want to, but it's worth a try. You come with me, Rosey. Jamie, you stay here with Cary in case they come back or the doctor arrives." "That'll be the day," he thought, "when he drives all the way out here and I have to tell him the patient's gone off with a girl of fourteen." As they got into the car, he said, "We'll have to tell the police."

It took five minues to drive along the lane. The lych gate was open as it had been three days before. Rosemary went to the stone where she'd found Veryan rehearsing death, but there was no one there. She and Bran looked behind monuments and tombs, around the edge of the small churchyard, where theirs were the first feet to crush the long wet grass. Bran called "Veryan!" and a cloud of dark birds clattered into the air from the bare tree in the lane beyond the gate, making them both start. But no voice called back.

"Was the church locked when you were here?" Bran asked.

"No. Do you think . . . ?"

The daylight seemed to have been drained away from the interior of the church and it was very still. Their feet sounded loud as they walked up the aisle, peering at the pews on either side. And nothing moved. Only when Bran again said, "Veryan!" just above a whisper was there an answering sound. From a pew beyond the side aisle, immediately under the memorial tablet which she and Rosemary had read together, Veryan said softly, "I'm here."

She was sitting at one end of the dark oak bench. As

they came nearer, she put her finger to her lips. Philip lay stretched full length along the bench beside her, his head on her lap. He lay quiet and relaxed, his face smooth and quiet, his breathing regular. Veryan whispered to Rosemary, "I couldn't tell you. But I knew you'd look for us here."

"But why? Why did you bring him here?" Rosemary whispered urgently back.

"I had to get him out of the house . . ."

"But why to the church?"

Veryan replied with only one word. "Sanctuary."

17

Two days later Rosemary went down to the village to see Nancy Rammage.

"We're leaving this afternoon. So could you stop the milk, please? And can I have the bill? We must owe you a lot."

"How's Mr. Philip?" the woman asked.

"They say at the hospital that he's going to be all right."

"That's good, then."

"They said he'd been asleep most of the time."

"Best thing for him," Nancy Rammage said. She was looking through papers hanging on a nail on the wall. Now she drew one out. "Here's your bill. Two pints was it, this morning?"

"That's right. And two yogurts."

Nancy Rammage ran her finger down the column of figures, adding. "That'll be twelve pound fifty-five and half all together, then."

As she gave Rosemary back the change, she asked, "Sorry to be going?" and Rosemary answered emphatically, "No," without stopping to think. Nancy Rammage smiled at her.

"It's not an easy house to live in," she said, as she'd said before.

"But I don't understand why. I mean, it's beautiful."

"Too beautiful. It's not right for the country around here."

"But it isn't just that."

Nancy Rammage said, "No?" making it a question. Rosemary looked at her and saw that she was serious, waiting for an explanation. Not thinking it was all stupid imagination.

"You said people here didn't ever live there. That they'd work there in the daytime. Why? Is it haunted or something?"

Nancy Rammage said scornfully, "For a place to be haunted, someone's got to have had some feelings there. Hasn't it?"

"Is that what's wrong? That it doesn't have feelings? Was there something terrible? I mean . . . the man who built the house? Was he wicked or something?"

"No one was wicked that I've ever heard," Nancy said. Then, as Rosemary began another question, she added, "Proud, maybe."

"What d'you mean, proud?"

"Building a house like that, in that place. That wasn't right. It's just an ordinary village, this. Nothing special. It doesn't need a house like that. More like a palace than a house, if you ask me."

"So what happened?" Rosemary asked.

"Nothing happened. Not the way you mean," Nancy Rammage said.

"How d'you mean, then? Nothing?"

"No babies. Not one of the Mr. Edmunds that lived there ever had a son born there to come after him. That for one thing."

"But . . . Philip's aunt. That was married to his uncle. She had a baby. It says so in the church," Rosemary said.

"And it killed her," Nancy Rammage said.

"Why? Do you know? What happened?"

"I don't know the whole story. She was all right at first, while she was carrying. She was so pleased. She said to my mother once, 'Mrs. Strong, do you know this is going to be the first baby that's been born here for more than a hundred years?' She was right to be pleased with herself. She thought she'd beaten the house and its ways."

"How, beaten the house?" Rosemary asked.

Nancy Rammage didn't answer this directly. She said, "If anyone could have done it, she would have, Mrs. Peter. Loving, that's what she was. But it wasn't to be. The house was stronger than her. Stronger than the baby, too, poor little thing."

196

Rosemary was silent, imagining the chilling end of the hopes which the lovely, loving lady had carried with the baby. She shivered. Nancy Rammage, watching her, said, "You and your friends felt it, didn't you? That it's just a house, like on show. Not a home."

"Yes. Only it was worse for Philip than for the rest of

"It would be. He's one of the family, isn't he?"

us."

He was also, Rosemary thought, the most susceptible of the six of them who had been staying there. He hadn't Cary's hardheadedness, he hadn't Bran's strong intention to be nothing but himself. He was more sensitive than Jamie, and he didn't have Veryan's strange, composed wisdom. She, Rosemary, was the most like Philip. But she, Rosemary, had had Bran.

"There's another tale they tell in the village. I daresay it's nothing but gossip. Though I know my mother believed it. And anyway, what would it matter so long as you got your sleep?"

"What wouldn't matter?" Rosemary didn't understand.

"They used to say no one couldn't dream up there. Well, most people couldn't. But I daresay that's all nonsense. And as I said, why should that harm anyone?"

Rosemary remembered Philip's "Not the right kind of sleep." She remembered Veryan saying, "I'm a very strong dreamer." It was true, she hadn't had a single dream in all the ten days they'd been staying in Winter's End. She hadn't even woken up knowing that she'd dreamed but forgotten what the dreams were about. She said, "There are places where you always dream more than usual," and Nancy Rammage said, "There might be something in it. I don't know. There are some funny things happen that no one can explain, even in this day and age. Anyway, you're going now, so you don't have to bother about it."

"No—o. Only it's still Philip's house."

"Might be seeing you again someday, then."

"I suppose so," Rosemary said. But she didn't mean ever to come back here. She turned towards the door. "I'd better get back. Thanks for everything."

"You're welcome."

" 'Bye!"

Puzzling. Rosemary wondered what Bran would make of it.

Bran, allowed into the side ward for a brief visit, found Philip asleep. Deeply asleep, lying on his side in the easy, relaxed position Bran had seen before when he'd lain under Veryan's care in the church two days before.

It seemed a pity to wake him. Bran sat down on the only chair and watched him. It was difficult to reconcile this peaceful figure with the frantic boy who had suspected everyone of conspiring against him. He lay almost completely still. Only now and then his eyelids trembled as if beneath them his dreaming eyes saw something invisible to the outside world.

After ten minutes, Bran got up to leave. But as he touched the handle of the door, Philip stirred and turned

198

over. His eyes opened and scanned the room, the window, and then Bran. He said, "Bran?" in a tone of faint surprise.

"Yes, it's me. Hi!"

Philip said, "Hi!" and lay still, looking at his visitor.

"Feeling all right?" Bran asked.

"Fine. A bit tired, that's all."

Bran sat down on the chair again.

"How long've I been here?" Philip said next.

"Two days." Bran didn't know how much Philip remembered or what he'd been told. He'd come with carefully prepared evasions in case he found himself questioned by a madman. He was relieved to find that these probably wouldn't be necessary.

"I didn't realize it was so long."

"You've been asleep most of the time," Bran said.

"Have I?"

"That's what the nurses told me."

Philip was silent for a time. Then he said, "What's happening to everyone?"

"We're leaving later this afternoon. Rosemary's been clearing up. I'm taking Veryan and Jamie to the station after lunch and then Rosey and I'll go back by car." He deliberately didn't mention Cary in case her name might be disturbing, but Philip asked, "What about Cary? How's she getting home?"

"We put her on a train yesterday." He didn't add that she had been as anxious to leave as they had to get rid of her.

"Poor Cary" was Philip's next remark.

"Why?" Bran asked cautiously.

"Why what?"

"Why did you say, 'Poor Cary'?"

Philip looked puzzled. "I'm not sure. I just felt sorry for her." He said suddenly, with the first signs of anxiety, "She's all right, isn't she?"

"Seemed all right when she went off."

"I thought . . . Trouble is I'm a bit muddled. I can't make out what really happened and what I've been dreaming. It all seems real. No, that's not right. I mean . . . nothing seems realer than anything else. I know some of the things are dreams, but they're just as real as things that really happened. Know what I mean?"

"Like what?"

"Like Veryan having that nightmare. That was real, wasn't it?"

"Like hell it was," Bran said with feeling.

"But just now I dreamed that I was in the house and I couldn't get out. None of the rest of you were there. You were all outside waiting for me. No, not Cary. She wasn't . . . anywhere. . . ."

"So what happened?"

"I got out. It was all right. But it's just as real as the other things. As real as being in here. As real as you." He smiled to show that he wasn't challenging Bran's solid reality.

"When do they say you'll be out?" Bran asked.

"Day after tomorrow. My mother's coming to fetch me."

"See you week after next, then. I'm glad you're so

200

much better. You look quite different," Bran said, preparing to leave.

"I feel different. All I needed was a lot of proper sleep."

"Well, get it, then. Only don't spend too much of it dreaming."

"I might need to," Philip said. Bran stared at him.

"What's that supposed to mean? You don't need to dream."

"The doctor here was telling me about people who don't dream enough. Did you know they've done experiments in the States? And if people are woken up whenever they start dreaming, they go funny. Sort of mad. Like I was."

"You can't really believe . . ." Bran began, but Philip interrupted him. "It's true, you know. I didn't have any dreams up at Winter's End. It could have been something to do with that. Couldn't it?"

"I suppose it could," Bran said, more to humor Philip than because he was at all convinced.

"Well, anyway. I dream all the time here," Philip said.

"I hope it does you good," Bran said, half joking.

"It does."

" 'Bye," Bran said at the door.

" 'Bye. Give my love to Rosemary."

"Sure. Be seeing you," Bran said, and left. Funny fellow, he thought. The same sweet-tempered, friendly boy he'd always seemed to be. So what was this episode all about? Jealousy? Primitive land envy? Or something

201

stranger, like this suggestion that Philip's personality could be changed if he didn't dream? What use were dreams, anyway? thought practical Bran. Much more likely to have been an infection. Philip had probably been running a fever, and none of them had noticed it. Bran's mum, though, would have put it all down to gut trouble. Indigestion and constipation were always the first things she thought of if any of the family weren't well. Not that she'd ever suffered from either herself, as far as he knew. But she was a great one for the simplest explanation of anything she didn't understand, and she was right, too, as often as not.

The cheese-for-supper explanation covered a lot of curious things. Bran laughed at himself for coming back to it. Then began to think about Rosey again, and drove the faster to get back to her.

Bran drew the car up outside the little station and while Jamie and Veryan struggled out of the back, he busied himself getting their luggage out of the boot.

" 'Bye, Rosemary. Have a good term. Only two weeks more till we go back. Christ, I've got such a lot to get through!" Jamie said.

" 'Bye, Jamie."

"Good-bye," Veryan said. She held out an awkward hand. On impulse, Rosemary put her arms around the girl and kissed her.

"Come and visit me?" she said.

"Could I? Wouldn't your . . . mother mind?"

"She'd love it. We've got masses of room now the boys have gone."

"I'd like to, then."

"I'll tell Mum." One thing about Mum, maddening though she could be in some ways, Rosemary thought, was that she'd always welcome their friends. Once she knew Veryan's history, it'd be a wonder if she didn't try to half adopt her. But that problem would have to be dealt with later. The train came shuddering in, the carriage doors flew open, Jamie and Veryan disappeared. Doors slammed, hands waved out of windows, faces were obscured, then gone. Only the empty track, lines leading off into infinity, always getting closer, never quite meeting. Rosemary and Bran returned to the car.

"What'll your mum make of that kid?" Bran asked as they drove off.

"She'll be all right. She won't fuss her."

"She's really in love with Philip. Don't you agree?"

"Why do you say so?"

"The way she looked at him when he was asleep. Poor bloody baby," Bran said, as he'd said before.

"Why? He might . . ."

"I don't think so. He doesn't think of her as anything except just Jamie's kid sister."

"But . . . she was the only person he listened to . . ."

"He listened to her just because she's a kid. Don't you see . . . ?"

"No. . . ."

"Because the rest of us were threatening him. One way or another. But Veryan . . . she's not old enough to want to keep him out of his own house. She's not old enough . . . that's what he thinks . . . to want to be his girl friend. She's like they say—children and fools tell the truth. So he trusts her. See?"

Rosemary said, "Poor Veryan!" as Veryan had once said, "Poor Philip!"

Bran put his spare arm around her shoulders and hugged her quickly before a tricky problem of overtaking necessitated his having both hands on the wheel.

"Rosey!"

"What, Bran?"

"Your mum. What's she going to make of me?"

But the answer to this is too complex for Rosemary to be able to answer at once. She sits silent beside Bran, watching the road rush towards her and slide under the car's wheels, still unfolding in front of her eyes, always changing, turning in this direction and that, bringing who knows what around the next bend. She tries to imagine what her mum will say if she takes Bran home with her. What her parents will find to say to Bran or he to them. Tries to imagine a life which encompasses both these totally different ways of thinking and being. Can she, Rosemary, hold them all together in her own person, be Rosemary, daughter, half committed to and half rebelling against one kind of life, and Rosemary, lover, possibly wife, promised to something different, alien? And how different are these ways? Is she, perhaps, really following the same path that her parents in their time had beaten for themselves? How much of the same goes on forever, in spite of the feeling that this is new, this is for me, they never knew what it was like to feel like this? How much of this is sex? Is it being in love? Who is going to answer this question? Not Mum, not Dad. Not Bran, even. Rosemary will have to discover this for herself.

To Bran, she says, "I don't know. Drive me home and see."

Up at Winter's End the window shades are drawn down over the bolted windows like eyelids over sleeping eyes. Around, the trees and shrubs are just coming into late flowering and the small green leaves are beginning to flutter from the dark branches. There are daffodils in the long grass. But the house is unaffected by the coming of spring, and it slumbers on. The rooms inside are silent and empty again; and now that the comforting warmth of the Rayburn has been cooled, the whole of the building is chilled. In sole possession now, Mrs. Eye scuttles from room to room, flicking away infinitesimal particles of dust from the marble mantelpieces and from the polished wood of the bookcase and cabinets. This is how she likes to see *her* house. Spotless, correct, immaculate; not a cushion out of place, not a crumb in the kitchen, not a crease on a pillow or a wrinkle in a counterpane. Only the kitchen, neat as it is, gives her a moment's uneasiness. Too lately it was warm, it was alive. She doesn't approve of the brown pottery mugs hanging in the dresser. She would have preferred white bone china cups.

But at least she can now keep the place as it should be kept. A place where no unsightly feelings are allowed to intrude. A clean, a sterile place. An orderly house, where no one laughs without good reason, and no one cries. A house where beauty must not be disturbed, where the turbulence of life and love and birth must be subdued for the sake of order. Winter's End. A white house. White for innocence, for ignorance. White for a sepulcher. White for death.

Format by Gloria Bressler
Set in Bodoni Book
Composed, printed and bound by Vail-Ballou Press, Inc.
HARPER & ROW, PUBLISHERS, INCORPORATED